THE CHRONICLES OF ELWIC

Published by Spines
ISBN: 979-8-89691-252-1

THE CHRONICLES OF ELWIC

TALES OF HAVENBROOK

DAN ARMSTRONG

CONTENTS

ADVANCED REVIEWS

This book, "Tales of Havenbrook," is a testament to the power of wisdom and virtue, a poignant reminder of how one individual can leave a lasting impact. It is a touching, thought-provoking read for anyone seeking both inspiration and introspection.

— CHRISTINA ALVA "USA TODAY" BEST-SELLING AUTHOR AND SPEAKER

Dan has done it again! A powerful story meets ancient wisdom with a fresh twist on making meaning while making money. Your financial IQ will soar to match your spiritual IQ, as true wealth lies in kindness and care for humanity. This timeless book's storytelling will captivate you while offering simple steps to truly flow in life. A must-read for anyone seeking both prosperity and purpose.

— SIMON T. BAILEY AUTHOR OF
RESILIENCE@WORK - HOW TO COACH
YOURSELF INTO A THRIVING FUTURE

Dan Armstrong is an amazing writer. I was enthralled by this story. Hidden within the story were so many biblical truths. I could visualize the different scenarios and, at times, felt that he was speaking directly to me. This book contains lots of life-changing nuggets of challenging wisdom. Great life lessons! I highly recommend this book.

— ETHEL RUCKER AUTHOR, PASTOR AND CO-
FOUNDER OF THE CHRISTIAN DEVELOPMENT
CENTER, CALIFORNIA.

Dan Armstrong has crafted a compelling book of wisdom for fiction lovers who value personal growth and seek deeper meaning in life. Each chapter presents relatable stories woven with life lessons, offering gentle reminders to acquire knowledge, share it, and act with courage. With opportunities for self-reflection and insights into finding contentment and fulfillment, this book is a must-read for anyone aspiring to live a purposeful life and embody the virtues they hold dear.

— BRANDY WILSON EDWARDS, ATTORNEY,
MOTIVATIONAL SPEAKER, AUTHOR AND WELL-
BEING ADVOCATE

Dan Armstrong delivers yet another masterpiece with "The Chronicles of Elwic: Tales of Havenbrook", a brilliant continuation of his previous work, The Chronicles of Elwic: The Temple of Wisdom and Truth. Once again, Dan invites readers on an extraordinary journey filled with profound insights, weaving timeless biblical truths with captivating parables that inspire deep thought.

This follow-up is more than a book—it's a guide to living a life grounded in love, compassion, and virtue. With each chapter, Dan masterfully balances wisdom and storytelling, offering lessons that resonate long after the final page. Expect the unexpected as Dan challenges readers to see life through a lens free of judgment, embracing a path of kindness and inner growth. Simply put, this is a literary gem—a must-read for anyone seeking truth, wisdom, and a richer way to navigate the world.

— ROBERT COMMODARI HOST OF THE
PODCAST "CHISELED," AUTHOR, SPEAKER,
AND BUSINESS OWNER.

In his latest work, The Chronicles of Elwic, Dan Armstrong brings to life the timeless village of Havenbrook, where virtues and values shape a community that is both mesmerizing and relatable. Armstrong's characters are vivid and multidimensional, each grappling with universal struggles—pride, envy, and the relentless pursuit of personal glory. This story offers a delicate balance of fantasy and reality, beckoning readers to reflect on their own lives and values. Armstrong's tale is more than an escape; it's a mirror reflecting the virtues we strive to uphold amidst the cacophony of daily life.

— TAMMY THRASHER MITCHELL

Once again, Dan Armstrong weaves words rich with timeless and poignant life lessons. Reading it only once would be a disservice to the depth of wisdom contained here. I found myself reading, re-reading, underlining, and absorbing the meaning of each lesson.

"The Circle of Virtue" is a timeless guide, and to single out just one or two lessons would overlook the wealth found throughout. The town of Havenbrook and the virtues displayed on flags outside each merchant's doorway add layers of beauty and meaning. This is a book to share—worth reading for both young and old alike.

— JOHN POTTS – FRISCO, TEXAS

"The Chronicles of Elwic: Tales of Havenbrook" engages readers from the very first page. The sage Elwic teaches all wisdom-seekers who come to the village of Havenbrook the virtues of humility, integrity, empathy, self-governance and the power of community through vivid and captivating parables that all can easily understand. A must-read!

— ALAN STEWART, REAL ESTATE INVESTOR &
4X BEST-SELLING AUTHOR. COFOUNDER OF
SAPIENT CAPITAL

INTRODUCTION

Between two majestic mountain ranges lies the once tranquil village of Havenbrook. Over time, it transformed into a magnet for seekers from all walks of life—a vibrant nexus of learning where social status held no sway. Here, the wealthiest nobles and the humblest peasants alike were welcomed without prejudice, invited to partake in a feast of knowledge, indulging in truths and savoring the nuggets of wisdom offered. None departed without feeling fulfilled, yet many found themselves drawn back, hungry for more. Some came out of sheer curiosity, while others approached with a deep reverence for the enigmatic aura that surrounded the village.

The streets, paved with cobblestones meticulously laid, echoed with the rapid footsteps of leather-clad travelers. The aroma of outdoor cooking mingled with the air, tantalizing the senses with its esoteric allure. Colorful flags adorned the entrances of shops, fluttering joyfully in the breeze, while the laughter of children spilled from open windows. In the marketplace, the hearty guffaw of a burly man reverberated between the wooden and stone structures. It was a bustling center of commerce and yet exuded an aura of serene tranquility, a paradox that intrigued all that passed through.

Legends of gaining profound wisdom from an ancient sage lured countless seekers to forsake their worldly possessions and embark on a pilgrimage to Havenbrook. Many felt irresistibly drawn to the village, as if compelled by some otherworldly force.

Now marked on maps as a town, Havenbrook boasted a rule of law, though violations were rare. Observing the bustling streets and vibrantly painted structures, one could scarcely imagine its humble origins as a poor and secluded village, scarcely noticed by merchants. Its transformation into a thriving town began with the return of the Sage, Elwic, from his own pilgrimage. Armed with newfound knowledge from the fabled Temple of Wisdom and Truth, he constructed the Tower using logs from his father's craft and established a school where education was not only free but also impossible to ignore. His words had the power to soften the hardest of hearts, challenge the proudest of souls, and provoke thought in all who dared to listen. And now, dear friend and seeker, read the tales of Havenbrook penned by the scribe Actar.

CHAPTER 1
SMALL STEPS

"A SPARK OF FEAR AND A HINT OF COURAGE CAN IGNITE THE HEART of anyone to change their world", Elwic declared, his cloak open to welcome the warmth of the fire. After dusk, the teachings of Elwic drew townsfolk and visitors alike to the nightly ritual, even during the rain, finding refuge within the Tower of Havenbrook's spacious confines. The hardened dirt floors were adorned with rugs, tokens of friendship from dignitaries and merchants who had once been strangers but now departed as friends, and some as family.

"Why do you seek to change your world?" Elwic's gaze fell upon a young traveler.

The traveler hesitated before responding. "Well, I... I find many in my village resistant to my suggestions. I offer them advice on improving their crafts."

"And do you practice the crafts you advise others on? Elwic inquired.

"I... I do not," the traveler lifted his chin defiantly, "But, I observe their work and believe I see ways to improve it."

Elwic shook his head gently. "There is indeed a spark of fear and a hint of courage within you that drives you to speak out. But, young one, if you wish to change the world, begin by mastering your own craft. Your concern for others will then become less burdensome. What is your craft?"

The young traveler hesitated, then spoke. "I am a wheelwright, and I meet all the trades in my village when they need me to fix their carts and wagons. I know what they do, and in my heart, I believe I can do it better than they can."

Elwic sighed, his eyes twinkling as he looked at the lad. "But have you worked as an apprentice in their trades? Have you sharpened the blade of a knifeman? Have you spun yarn from the wool of sheep? Do you own the abacus of a taxman?"

"I have not and do not, but I can see!" the traveler declared boldly, lifting his chin in defiance.

A few chuckles and nudges in the crowd chipped away at the traveler's confidence.

"The passion to change the world is commendable," Elwic continued, "but it must start with the self. Pay heed to your own heart before seeking to guide others. Your appearance as a young one betrays the experience you lack. I would suggest asking permission rather than offering advice." Elwic nodded at the boy and smiled.

A hush fell over the crowd as Elwic concluded his teaching. The young traveler, though embarrassed, was moved by the sage's words and quietly slipped into the darkness of the night.

"Humility," Elwic continued, "Humility is the cornerstone of true wisdom. One must empty oneself of pride and arrogance. There is no shame in admitting ignorance, but it is shameful to pretend knowledge one does not possess." His words were not directed at any individual but invited self-reflection.

"Though you may perceive me as wise, I am but a humble servant of knowledge. Beware those who claim to possess all the answers. Their foundation is not humility but pride, and it will crumble beneath them. Better to be naked and alive than clothed and buried beneath the rubble of their falsehoods. Avoid those who proclaim themselves prophets or seers of the future. Look at the trail of destruction they leave in their wake."

"Dear Sage", a voice cried out. "I am a merchant, toiling daily in my trade. Yet, there is one in my town who possesses great wealth, a treasure beyond my wildest dreams. How can I approach him and convince him to share his fortune with me?"

Elwic listened intently before responding. "When you arrived in Havenbrook, where did you venture first? Did you seek shelter in an inn or peruse the marketplace? How did you spend your initial hours?"

The merchant chuckled, "Well, I was parched! I sought a drink, heading straight for the nearest alehouse. One must quench their thirst before tending to business!" His words elicited laughter and approval from the crowd, basking in his charismatic charm.

"And does this wealthy fellow citizen of yours frequent the alehouse?" Elwic inquired.

"I couldn't say. I've never spotted him there," the merchant admitted.

Elwic nodded knowingly. "Therein lies your answer."

The crowd fell silent as Elwic continued, "And how do you spend your leisure time after work?"

The merchant hesitated. "As much as I have... well, here, enjoying myself at the alehouse."

"And do you not spend your earnings there?" Elwic pressed.

The merchant shifted uncomfortably. "Well, yes, the ale isn't free," he conceded, expecting a chuckle from the audience. Silence was the answer.

"Why concern yourself with another's riches when you squander the precious hours at your disposal?"

Elwic's gaze bore into the merchant, the smirk fading from his face. "Each hour spent, and every coin dropped in the alehouse never returns—instead, they vanish. Do you relieve yourself in the alley behind the alehouse? You have wasted the gift of time and the weight of silver as it spills on the dirt, lost forever. Perhaps your portion in life is as it stands. Perhaps the Spirit deems you capable of bearing only what you possess. Elwic paused, assessing the merchant's comprehension. "Do you have bread to eat, ale to drink, and clothes to wear?"

The merchant stuttered, "Yes, yes, I do."

"Then you are wealthier than every soul laid to rest," Elwic declared. "You are alive, breathing, seeing, hearing, walking, and speaking. Your wealth surpasses material riches. Leave thoughts of another's fortune to burn in this fire, and let its light guide you toward a new path. Seek inspiration from your fellow citizens; ask, and you may receive. There is always more to share than we can create. Small steps lead to great leaps unseen by many."

The merchant stared into the flames. The air was hot, but the lesson was warm and comforting. Time is valuable. Do not envy. Work on yourself. Create, do not compete. Look within, not without. One small step leads to great rewards. Use the faculties you have. Being alive is wealth. Ask, and it shall be given. Seek, and you will find.

He nodded. He was ready to take what he had, use it wisely, and honor the gifts the Spirit had given him. "Dear Sage of Havenbrook, I say to you today, I shall return with a payment for your words. I am the reason I am, and I will use your tongue's words to change my lot. You will see!"

Elwic responded, "Seek first to learn and serve, and then all the wealth you deserve will be added to your purse."

The merchant smiled; his heart was overjoyed. He had come to the town with a burden and left with a blessing. His heart was filled with hate, but now he was being healed. The jealous thoughts were turned to joyous revelations of life and liberty. He would learn the ways of wealth from those he dishonored with rumors and false accusations. He would no longer be the judge and jury of others' success but rather a student with a passion for information.

He heard his inner voice. "You are no longer a victim. You can speak the voice of victory. Ruminate on the words that wage war with your old ways and let them wash the wasted years from your life."

He had spent too much time glaring and staring at the success of another, and too little asking what he could do better.

The Sage of Havenbrook spoke directly to his soul. The toll was paid, a new path would begin, and all who heard the words of Elwic would awaken the next day to a brighter world. Every small step was a move in the vision of each one's calling. Until then, the fire fizzled to ashes, and the town fell asleep.

CHAPTER 2

THE CIRCLE OF VIRTUE

IT WAS TRULY REMARKABLE TO WITNESS THE METAMORPHOSIS OF Havenbrook, evolving from a humble village inhabited by a handful of families into a bustling town teeming with a diverse array of tradespeople and vendors. Beyond merely a geographical location, Havenbrook was fast becoming a sought-after destination. Elwic's renown spread far and wide, shrouded in mystique for some. Initially dismissed as mere folklore, tales of his wisdom and teachings gained credence as first-hand witnesses attested to his mortal existence.

The existence of a school in such an outlying area raised eyebrows, prompting skepticism from those residing in more traditional brick homes and stone fortifications. "Surely," they scoffed, "people wouldn't flock to heed a prophet in such a remote corner of the region."

Yet, against all odds, it was undeniably true. Visitors embarked on journeys to seek out the town of Havenbrook, bringing many goods for trade: spices, dried fruits, vibrant textiles, tools, and myriad artisanal skills— from tannery to shoemaking, from masonry to other crafts— enriched the burgeoning community. As these travelers opted to settle down, they erected huts and engaged in bartering for sustenance until their respective crafts found favor among the townsfolk.

With each passing day, Havenbrook's borders expanded, and its fields transformed into a majestic patchwork of crops yielding abundant produce previously foreign to the village. Knowledge turned out to be the catalyst for prosperity as education took root in the minds of a select few, the fruits of which were savored by all who embraced and disseminated the teachings of Elwic, the Sage of Havenbrook.

"That flag adorning your doorway is quite striking!" remarked Anika, the herbalist specializing in teas, gesturing toward the fluttering banner proudly affixed to a wooden branch. "Ah, yes! It's the flag of Honesty," replied the shopkeeper with pride. "This week, it's my honor to fly it high."

Anika's smile widened as she recounted the heartening tale. A shoemaker, deeply moved by the notion that honesty could be the linchpin for business growth, resolved to craft a flag bearing the emblem of honesty and proudly display it outside his shop. The symbolism resonated deeply within the community, prompting several other merchants to follow suit. Soon, flags representing various virtues began to dot the once drab brown and gray streets, infusing them with a vibrant tapestry of colors and cheer.

She fondly recalled the council meeting held around a crackling bonfire, where the elders proposed a flag ceremony. After each trading week, the flags would be rotated among the burgeoning town, serving as a visual reminder of the virtues they represented. Inspired by the virtue displayed above their doors for the week, shop owners endeavored to embody it in their business dealings. Daily glimpses of these flags before entering their places of trade instilled the truths deep within their consciousness. The tangible evidence of virtue practice manifested in the expansion of their profits and the tranquility of their souls.

"I still remember when the flag of Compassion was hoisted above my shop," the shoemaker reflected with a rueful shake of his head. "I was once selfish, scorning the beggar who sought alms door to door. I even callously drenched his feet with dirty water. What a despicable act!" His voice trailed off as he felt the weight of past transgressions settle upon him.

"By the middle of the week, after immersing myself in the symbol day and night, I realized my deficiency in practicing compassion. Seeking solace, I approached Elwic, beseeching forgiveness. His response was simple yet profound: 'There is grace in the morning.' He neither condemned nor chastised me for my shortcomings. True to his word, the beggar passed by my shop the next morning. Though he avoided direct contact, I beckoned him with a smile and offered him a loaf of bread. As he accepted the gift, he offered words of gratitude." The shopkeeper sighed deeply; his gaze distant as he pondered the transformative power of compassion.

"Had it not been for the flag of Compassion serving as a poignant reminder, my heart might still be hardened toward the less fortunate in our town. I am grateful for the weekly saturation of Elwic's teachings, which continue to guide me on the path of virtue."

Anika's heart swelled with emotion upon hearing the story. "I, too, was once touched by the flag of Compassion," she confessed. "It transformed my heart." She recounted an incident from many weeks prior, when a frail merchant promised to trade fruit for her tea, only to fail to deliver it after Anika had already handed over her precious blend. "I was consumed with anger and sought her out," Anika admitted, her tone tinged with remorse.

She bowed her head in shame and continued, "I found her living in a shanty near the woods. Rage coursed through me, ready to unleash a torrent of curses upon her. But then I saw a small child in her arms, sipping the tea I had given her—a special blend for internal pain. At her feet lay a bag of berries, rightfully mine. As she looked up at me, her eyes pleaded for forgiveness. At that moment, I realized my judgment had been harsh and unfounded. She wasn't a thief but a mother desperate to care for her child. If she had taken the time to bring the berries into town, it could have spelled the death of her baby. Oh, how I begged for forgiveness for my indifference and callousness."

The shoemaker leaned in, captivated. "What happened next?" he inquired eagerly.

Anika's eyes sparkled with pride and astonishment as she continued her tale. "I'll tell you what happened! She handed over the berries and I marched back into town and sold them. I recounted the story when the buyer questioned why I was selling instead of keeping them for myself. He was so moved by the tale that he tripled what he initially offered, declaring it an act worthy of honor. And so, the flag of Honor flew proudly above his shop."

"With the money," Anika exclaimed, "I went straight to the cloth shop. I requested as much heavy cloth as my payment could afford. When they questioned my sudden interest in cloth, I recounted the story. Touched by the narrative, they generously gave me enough heavy fabric to cover a castle!"

"As I left the cloth shop," Anika concluded, a triumphant smile gracing her lips, "I glanced up and saw a flag of virtue proudly displayed above the carpenter's door."

"Pray tell! What flag of virtue was displayed?" The shoemaker's curiosity bubbled forth like that of an eager child.

"Ha! It was Generosity," Anika exclaimed, her voice tinged with astonishment, prompting laughter from the shoemaker. Sensing his interest, she eagerly continued her tale.

"Now, I went to the carpenter and relayed, 'I've been sent from the cloth maker to share a story with you.' He was taken aback. I had not realized he was indebted to the cloth maker. As I recounted my journey from merchant to merchant, his heart broke. Tears welled in his eyes. 'I owe the cloth maker,' he confessed, 'and now, with the Kindness and Love of my fellow citizens of Havenbrook, I shall build a hut for the woman and the child. The collective generosity of our community will cover their shelter. Go and convey to them that my home is theirs until I complete their dwelling.'"

Anika paused, overcome with what had transpired in mere hours. "I felt a surge of energy in my soul, a vitality I hadn't known since my youth," she recounted, her voice filled with gratitude. "As I thanked the carpenter, he insisted, 'No! Please — do not thank me. The flag of Dignity has flown over my door for a week, yet I despaired of ever fulfilling my obligation to this virtue. But you have restored not just my Compassion, Honor, and Generosity but also my Dignity. Now, I fulfil my debt to the cloth maker, for he has shown me Forgiveness.'"

Anika gazed into the shoemaker's eyes, her eyes shining with a fervent belief in the transformative power of practicing virtues. "Do you see, Shoemaker? Can you grasp how the teachings of the Sage of Havenbrook have imbued each of us with a deeper sense of purpose?" She paused, allowing the weight of her words to sink in. "Every act of virtue strengthens another. We are not merely observing symbols; we are embodying them. We are the living manifestations of these virtues!"

The shoemaker, his eyes wide with wonder, was rendered speechless, his throat dry as he swallowed hard, unable to articulate his astonishment. He could only nod in silent agreement.

"I wasted no time, I tell you!" Anika exclaimed, "I raced to the shanty in the woods where the woman and child resided, barely pausing to catch my breath upon arrival. At first, I found myself overcome with uncontrollable laughter. She must have thought me quite mad, returning on the same day with news of the redeemed trade, yet here I was, laughing with unbridled joy at the miraculous turn of events! Oh, it was laughter born of pure delight! I stood there with medicine for her child, cloth to clothe them, and a home to shelter them. As I recounted the tale to her, my enthusiasm was tempered by reverence; her response was stunned silence. Her eyes, wide as a startled deer, held an intense stillness. She was the unwitting beneficiary of many virtues practiced by a select few who had never even known her name."

The shoemaker listened in rapt attention; his awe evident. "I had heard whispers of the carpenter's humble abode in the shanty," he confessed. "But I never understood why. It all makes sense now. He is fulfilling his promise, just a few steps down this path from my shop." Pausing, he rubbed his chin thoughtfully before a spark of inspiration illuminated his features.

"Anika," he exclaimed, leaning in eagerly, "I have an idea."

"Yes?" Anika leaned in; her curiosity piqued.

"When the carpenter returns to his home, and the woman and child move into their new home, we must celebrate," the shoemaker declared with conviction. "And what better way to mark the occasion than with a sacred tea of dedication? Your tea, Anika—your mint and lilac blend—shall be served to all the citizens as they welcome the new family. And as for the cost, whatever it may be, it shall be my honor to cover it. You have exemplified the teachings of Elwic with grace and integrity, and your reward, my dear friend, is not something contrived or imagined; it is justly deserved. I offer you my blessing here and now!"

And so, it was in the town of Havenbrook. As the community wholeheartedly embraced the practice of virtues imparted by the Sage and was daily reminded by the flags—symbols imbued with deep meanings—Havenbrook flourished, strengthened by their collective commitment to serving one another. Indeed, many more chapters of this remarkable tale are to be known and heard. All things align for the greater good of those who attune their ears to the Spirit.

The awaited day dawned when the woman and child entered their new abode. Two neatly made beds of straw awaited them, adorned with numerous blankets that added warmth to the sleeping quarters and the walls. A wooden door proudly displayed the family's name, marking their rightful place within the community. With joyous hearts, the townsfolk congregated to celebrate, welcoming the new family into their midst. Outside, a vat of tea bubbled and steamed, its fragrant aroma filling the air as all gathered to partake in a ceremony of shared delight, sipping from cups filled with Anika's cherished mint and lilac tea.

With the completion of the tea-for-fruit trade, Anika was rewarded many times over, receiving over a hundredfold the value of her original exchange. The widow and the orphan found solace and shelter within the embrace of their new home, while the longstanding debt between the cloth maker and the carpenter was settled. Through these interconnected acts of kindness and reciprocity, the town of Havenbrook deepened its appreciation for the timeless wisdom emanating from the Tower, as imparted by the Sage of Havenbrook. Indeed, their journey of growth and enlightenment had only just begun.

CHAPTER 3

WALK WITHOUT SIGHT

"IF YOU EARNESTLY DESIRE PURITY, BRACE YOURSELF TO ENDURE ridicule for your choice. Even if your actions, born of righteous thoughts, align with your aspirations, there will always be those who seek to harm you. It's not your righteousness they detest; rather, it's their own afflictions that bind them. Everyone wishes you success until you surpass them. Your achievements shine a light on their failures. Instead of focusing on their darkness, stay committed to your own path."

A wandering scribe once transcribed these words during a session at the bonfire outside the tower of Havenbrook. He took the parchment and shared its teachings in his own village. The message eventually reached the ears of Cedric, a young and ambitious merchant who was also a skilled blacksmith. Cedric's expertise lay in crafting battleaxes from copper and wood, which were gaining popularity over swords, leading to the success of his business. Despite his proficiency in creating weapons, Cedric struggled with the moral implications of their eventual use. Though soldiers sought his axes and paid handsomely for them, Cedric found himself conflicted about profiting from conflict.

That fateful night, as he listened to the scribe recite the scroll, every word felt like a soothing balm to his soul. His thirst for knowledge only grew stronger, surpassing the heat of the coals that breathed life into his craft. The words of a distant teacher seemed to possess a power beyond anything Cedric had ever encountered. He knew he had to seek out this sage.

Upon learning of Elwic's reputation for guiding others toward prosperity, Cedric felt a glimmer of hope. He longed to uncover the secrets of wisdom that led to true wealth. With a few days of preparation, Cedric embarked on his quest to find the legendary "Sage of Havenbrook."

After weeks of arduous travel, Cedric finally stumbled upon the quaint town rumored to be Elwic's residence. As he approached, the sight of the tower overlooking the bustling community filled him with excitement. "It is just as the scribe described!" he exclaimed. Drawing nearer, Cedric felt a strange sense of assurance and safety, as if he were under some protective cloak. The colorful array of banners and flags lining the streets welcomed him after his journey through perilous mountain passes and treacherous roads.

Entering the first street, Cedric observed the houses and huts seeming to sway in harmony, as if greeting him in a silent song. Enchanted by the invisible music resonating within his soul, he spoke aloud, "What magical place is this where even the rocks and wood exude peace?" Knowing there would be no answer, he chuckled softly, acknowledging the whimsy of his query. The street, devoid of movement except for the dancing flags, seemed to beckon him onward, all pointing toward the towering structure ahead.

With a grin, Cedric addressed the fluttering cloths adorned with enigmatic symbols, "Very well, I shall follow your lead to the tower." His laughter carried on the breeze as he fixed his gaze on the goal before him.

Just ahead of him, amid the town square, Cedric noticed a gathering around a figure. Though he was clad in a tattered tunic, the voice from within the wool carried warmth and authority. It was none other than Elwic, passionately expounding on the intricate relationship between wealth and wisdom. Cedric couldn't help but marvel at the serendipitous timing of his arrival.

Intrigued, Cedric joined the audience, his attention captured by Elwic's captivating tales of ancient kingdoms, prosperous merchants, and wise rulers. Elwic's words resonated deeply with Cedric as he spoke of the significance of knowledge acquisition and personal development in attaining true wealth, which surpassed material possessions and required a profound understanding of oneself and the world. These were insights Cedric had never encountered before, causing him to reflect on his own spending habits and how he guarded his wealth.

"Sow the seeds of what you have earned into quarters, though not of equal measure," Elwic advised, his gaze scanning the crowd for any signs of dissent. Finding none, he continued, "First, allocate ten percent to the vulnerable— the weak, the widow, and the orphan within your kingdom. Whether it be aiding a neighbor in need, making a charitable donation to the temple or school, or supporting those who have enriched your life through their teachings. Secondly, reserve another ten percent, safeguarding it in a place where its temptation to be spent frivolously is minimized."

Pausing briefly, Elwic continued with conviction, "The next ten percent is to be entrusted to the marketplace, placed in the hands of skilled traders and merchants who possess the acumen to multiply wealth, thereby ensuring a return on your investment. The remaining seventy percent should address your basic needs— shelter, sustenance, clothing, and tools essential for survival. These principles are not only for personal growth but also serve to nourish the community at large. By caring for oneself, one naturally extends care to others. However, selfishness and hoarding of wealth lead to its eventual disappearance; it takes flight like a bird. One must sow before reaping, just as a fire requires a log to burn and warm a home, so it is with the principle of wealth. Feed the flame, and the flame will bring its reward."

As Elwic concluded his speech, Cedric approached him with a glimmer of hope in his eyes, attempting to steady his racing heart with deep breaths to no avail. Instead, he found himself calling out, "Esteemed Sage of Havenbrook, I humbly beseech you for an audience."

Elwic barely spared a glance at Cedric, and without a thought, gestured for him to follow. Cedric was taken aback by the unexpected hospitality. "Could he have foreseen my arrival?" Cedric wondered in a hushed tone. As the crowd parted, Cedric proceeded through the throng toward the tower, where Elwic, the Sage, gradually faded from view into the entrance. Cedric followed, making his way to the towering entrance arches, their heights surpassing that of a man. Taking a deep breath, he stepped into the shadow, closing his eyes and pressing forward in faith.

"Why have you come, young man?" Elwic's voice echoed faintly from within the gray chamber, barely audible.

"I've come to seek your guidance. I am a blacksmith with a skill worthy of good pay, yet I lack the wisdom to manage my earnings effectively. I wish to learn how to master my wealth rather than be controlled by it," Cedric replied, leaning forward, his eyes straining to discern the Sage's location within the darkness.

"Come closer," Elwic instructed softly. "Walk toward my voice. Darkness does not rule you."

Cedric hesitated momentarily, then steeled himself and moved forward. "Dear Sage of Havenbrook, I implore you, reveal yourself," Cedric pleaded.

With a grunt, Elwic whispered, "If you do not trust the teacher, you cannot be a student." Cedric stepped forward and trusted the still small voice. He walked where he could not see.

Elwic pulled back a curtain to reveal himself standing amidst flickering candles. His face remained shadowed, the candlelight casting dancing shadows upon his features. "Come, sit with me," Elwic invited, indicating a wooden bench. "I have some bread and honey."

As Cedric settled onto the bench, he felt as though he had entered sacred ground. Despite the packed dirt beneath his feet, he felt as though he were walking on air. The air was filled with the sweet fragrance of frankincense, and as his eyes adjusted to the dimness, he beheld the majesty of the room. The circular walls embraced him, wooden beams ascending inward until they met at a central point. Above, swirls of spent incense smoke filled the voluminous space, while candles mounted on upright logs at varying heights cast warm, flickering light throughout the room. Though shrouded in darkness, the dancing flames seemed undaunted by the challenge of illuminating the chamber with an ethereal glow. As Cedric breathed in the atmosphere of tranquility, he felt a sense of peace seep into his very being, enveloping him in its embrace.

"Please, sit, and let us talk," Elwic offered.

As Cedric savored the simple fare of bread and honey, a profound sense of peace enveloped him. He settled onto the thick rug before Elwic, meeting his gaze with unwavering trust. "I trust you," Cedric affirmed.

Elwic's smile deepened, his weathered cheeks creasing with warmth. "We have much to uncover," he replied.

CHAPTER 4
WALKING OUT WEALTH

"The art of patience," Elwic began, pausing to gauge Cedric's attention, "is akin to a canvas that requires time to dry." He stroked his beard thoughtfully, leaning forward in his seat. "True wealth," he continued, "is not attained quickly, nor should it be squandered in a single season."

"Please elaborate," Cedric requested, caught off guard by the enigmatic language.

"Let us begin with the canvas," Elwic suggested, smiling at Cedric, who returned a nod of curiosity.

"A layer of paint must be absorbed by the canvas before another layer can be applied," Elwic explained. "Is it not crucial to wait until the base can support the weight of additional color?"

Cedric lowered his head, his eyes welling with tears. "I do not comprehend, Sir Elwic," he confessed. "I yearn to understand. Please, bear with me, for I am young and restless, impatient with the passage of time."

"I understand," Elwic reassured him. "Impatience often leads to recklessness, particularly with newfound wealth. You see, Cedric, those who acquire riches prematurely often lack the wisdom to preserve them."

"And what of me? Am I foolish?" Cedric interjected.

"Are you?" Elwic countered gently. "Ask yourself why wealth slips through your fingers, seeking refuge in the hands of older merchants."

Cedric pondered the question, tilting his head in thought.

"Listen," Elwic urged. "When the trade is concluded, and gold or silver rests in your palm, do you grasp the significance of what has transpired?"

"Yes, I profit," Cedric replied, "and yet, no, because it slips away. Wealth evades my grasp like vapor, taunting me as I try to seize it. I am mocked."

"Yes, and it always will be until you grasp that wealth is merely a reflection of your character and your dedication to serving the masses. The canvas of opportunity is open to all, yet only a few seize the brush and the paint to leave their mark. But you, Cedric, you have dared where timid souls hesitate. It's better to attempt and fail than never to start and succeed. Your mistake lies in impatience, in not allowing the canvas to dry before rushing to paint anew. Your eagerness to reap before the harvest has matured has cost you lasting prosperity. Time is the currency of genius. It nurtures the seeds of skill and energy, providing sustenance for the hungry. Like a fruit with seeds of eternal bounty, each seed holds the potential for countless apples. Yet, you, young Cedric, have been harvesting before your crop reaches its full potential. The art of patience is as crucial as letting the canvas dry."

As Cedric pondered these words, he realized his folly in hasty profits and immediate gratification. His wealth had evaporated like mist in the morning sun, leaving him yearning for a greater yield. With a glance of desperation at Elwic, he posed the question, "What should I do?"

"When I speak of 'waiting for the canvas to dry,' I mean you should acknowledge your gains and then wait. While the money is still fresh in your hands, you spend it hastily. This money is fluid; it needs time to solidify so you can handle and manage it. Do not rush to decide how to use it until you have slept on it for thirty nights. Write down your needs and even your desires, then wait. If you let time pressure you, separating your list from the movement of the sun and moon, you'll realize that true needs are met while wants are thieves stealing from your future self. The older version of yourself is a simpler reflection of your present. Understand that nothing is permanent; everything is temporary. All things are yours now, yet nothing should constrain you. Your life is fleeting, like a mist or a flickering candle. And yet, you worry about wealth? Shouldn't you concern yourself with what you leave behind for the betterment of future generations? Are you so self-centered as to believe your life benefits over others? If so, your time is wasted. Let the paint dry on the canvas of your work, your labor, and especially your life! Building wealth is commendable, but it's noble to create a storehouse where others lack the skill. Think of what bread and wine can be yours before they spoil. Share with those who lack knowledge for now, but teach one if they are willing to learn. Do not withhold the wisdom you've gained and applied. Be a polished mirror for others to see the knowledge you've acquired. Like a candle's wick is a gateway for a flame, it is your chance to expand beyond your limits; a beacon for the less fortunate to see possibilities. The wick is the beginning of expanding your horizons. Cedric, you have the potential to grow and sustain the fruits of your passion. Take my words to heart; plant them, and with careful and patient observation, see the results align with their cause."

Cedric gasped for breath, his heart and soul pulsating with newfound purpose. Never had his mind felt so illuminated as it did on this enchanted night. He resolved to scrutinize his plans, practices, and objectives with renewed vigor. No longer would the meaningless pursuit of wealth consume him, squandered on trivial indulgences. Cedric embraced the conviction that true wealth transcended the hoarding of gold or silver in a dark vault; it was an embodiment of his life—a dynamic conduit for the betterment of others. He pledged to acquire and embody the virtues of patience, benevolence, and the imperative of imparting wealth to others through education.

Observing the transformation in his protégé's demeanor, Elwic felt compelled to impart one final admonition. "Cedric, resist the allure of opulent tents, golden rings, or robes of rare fabric, for their cost exceeds their value. Allow me to reiterate my teachings. Divide your earnings into quarters, though not necessarily of equal measure. First, allocate ten percent to support the weak, the widowed, and the orphaned within your realm—whether they be neighbors in need or contributions to temples, schools, or mentors. Secondly, set aside an additional ten percent in a secure reserve, ensuring its preservation from frivolous spending. Thirdly, invest ten percent in the marketplace, entrusting it to skilled traders and merchants who can nurture its growth and yield returns. Finally, allocate seventy percent to sustain your basic needs—shelter, sustenance, clothing, footwear, and tools essential for survival. Understand that these allocations serve not only your personal growth but also enrich the vitality of your community. By attending to your own welfare, you demonstrate the capacity to care for others. Conversely, selfish hoarding will lead to the dissipation of wealth, as it takes flight like a bird. Remember, one must sow before reaping rewards. Just as a fire requires fuel to burn, your daily toil precedes the warmth of the hearth. Place the log in place as a sacrifice before the expectation of heat."

"I am deeply grateful, dear Sage of Havenbrook. How can I ever repay you?" Cedric inquired with genuine humility.

Elwic reached within his tunic, producing a scroll. "Within this scroll lie the principles we've discussed, along with additional wisdom to satiate your hunger for knowledge. Study them diligently and impart their teachings to those receptive to learning. While you may still grapple with past missteps and immaturity, as you absorb and share these lessons, they will become ingrained in the fabric of your life. Stay resolute and practice daily. Resist temptation, and it shall retreat from you. Your former habits, which you've valiantly struggled against, shall henceforth wither away, no longer holding sway over you. Instead, may your pursuit of wealth become a conduit for blessing others, fulfilling the purpose of your calling. Go forth, Cedric, destined for prosperity, so you may broaden the horizons of the lands you traverse. Your reward shall be commensurate with the service you render."

With humility, Cedric accepted the scroll, bowing reverently to his teacher. "I shall be the unwavering student of your wisdom. May I never again doubt your guidance! Though the path may seem obscure, I will faithfully follow the teachings until the light within illuminates my way."

Tucking the scroll into his tunic, Cedric retrieved a gold coin from his purse, presenting it to Elwic. "This gold was meant for my journey's provisions, but I surrender it to you."

Elwic smiled warmly, reaching into a nearby bowl to retrieve nine silver coins. "Your understanding is profound. In exchange for your gold coin, I offer you nine silver coins. You have sown with your heart, which is the wealth of your soul. I return to you nine pieces of silver, and therefore, you have given freely ten percent in wisdom and truth. Now, go forth and embody the Cedric you are destined to become.

Over the years, Cedric blossomed into a sagacious and prosperous merchant, revered for his integrity and insight. While amassing considerable wealth, he also became a beacon of knowledge and inspiration for those seeking success. Cedric dutifully shared Elwic's teachings with aspiring entrepreneurs and scholars, imparting the invaluable lessons he had gleaned. In doing so, Cedric became a conduit for change. He became a beacon in the darkness, lighting the way for others to forge their own paths to success.

In the solitude of his tower, Elwic's gaze fixated on the dancing flame of a candle, his thoughts drifting back to his encounter with the seeker. With a gentle smile, he softly uttered, "You have become a wick, the origin of hope where a spark can ignite a flame to illuminate the world. Cedric, I stand with you."

CHAPTER 5

THE SCROLL OF WISDOM

FOR EVERY COIN YOU EARN OR ACQUIRE, DIVIDE IT INTO QUARTERS, acknowledging they are not equal in value. First, allocate ten percent to support the weak, the widowed, and the orphaned within your kingdom. The second ten percent should be set aside, saved in a secure place that discourages impulsive spending. Next, invest ten percent in the marketplace, entrusting it to skilled traders and merchants who can multiply your wealth and yield returns. Finally, allocate seventy percent to meet your basic needs: shelter, food, clothing, footwear, and tools essential for survival. Let this sacred scroll unveil the insights that guide the wise in the art of wealth. As destiny's quill dances upon this parchment, may its words etch themselves into the hearts of those seeking prosperity. True abundance is not solely measured in material gain but also in alignment with the virtues of care and responsibility. Without a pure heart and conscience, wealth will fade and pass. The wealth of the wicked is safeguarded for the wise until a Day of Reconciliation. Temper your accumulation with respect and mindfulness. Guard it as a hen covers her eggs, ready to release the fruit of its purpose with joy. Use it wisely and with contentment, never driven by insatiable desire. When death claims the temporal life and the grave embraces the mortal coil, mind this truth - all that is gathered in the dust of your castle is worthless to you. Therefore, heed the call to grow and give while you live. Your descendants will honor and revere your legacy for all you have accomplished.

I. The Nature of Currency

Behold the currency of kingdoms and empires—money, the tangible embodiment of value, a sacred instrument for commerce and comfort. Treat it with reverence, yet never elevate it to the status of worship. Remember, you are the master, and it shall never be your master. Understand its essence—a representation of labor, a symbol of trust. Like a flowing river, currency circulates, bringing life and sustenance to those who hold it. However, like a stagnant pond devoid of fresh water, stagnant money can lead to stagnation and decay. Keep it in motion; keep it vibrant, for as it flows, it grows. Regard it as a seed and a fruit, a reward for diligent effort. Assist it in cultivating its value by abstaining from frivolous pursuits such as gambling and careless spending on fleeting pleasures. Money can be a worthy adversary when managed with skill and prudence, yet a cruel mocker when indulged with greed or sloth. It serves as a mirror reflecting the soul of a man or a woman. Where your heart resides, there lies your treasure. Ensure your heart is pure, and your treasure shall endure. For if your heart is corrupted, every treasure becomes fleeting. I reiterate - guard the purity of your heart above all else.

II. Earn with Honor

Profit is indeed a noble pursuit. Without it, commerce and trade would falter, leaving laborers adrift as merchants lack the means to expand and offer more goods to the market. However, while greed can corrupt currency, turning it into a tool of evil, profit can also be wielded wisely or foolishly. Therefore, engage in labor that enriches the spirit and benefits the community. Like bees gathering nectar, accumulate wealth through diligence, honesty, and integrity. If within your capability, it is your duty to build wealth; if not, do not berate your limitations, but rather seek to learn from the wealthy until you too can attain prosperity. And if wealth remains elusive, serve others, so your needs are met, finding solace in the knowledge that the burdens of the affluent are not yours to bear. Earn with honor so that your soul may be enriched, and your heart finds peace.

Cursed is the one who amasses great riches yet finds no solace or trust in their abundance. Cursed is the one whose barns overflow while their inner self remains impoverished. It is better to earn a humble meal of potatoes than to feast on fruits and meats that spoil without the blessing of companionship. Earn with honor, and your days will be enriched by the company of friends and family. A coin earned through virtuous toil becomes a guiding light illuminating the path to prosperity, safeguarding your wealth within and without. Remember: "As within, so without."

III. Charity as Currency of the Soul

When the symphony of wealth plays its melody, let the tune of generosity harmonize with the chorus of philanthropy. Share the blessings bestowed upon you, for in giving, you receive the truest riches—the warmth of touched hearts, the echoes of gratitude. The currency of kindness transcends material possessions, weaving a tapestry of compassion. For every measure of earning, set aside a tenth without hesitation. Withholding a portion is akin to robbing opportunity from the very source that bestowed the gift. Talent, skill, or potential granted to you is a ripple in the vast ocean of life. Ignoring a seed does not absolve one of the responsibilities for its growth. The abundance is evident; even your family is included. Share the blessings. Give a tenth of all you have earned and witness prosperity flourish in the fields of gratitude, fortune, joy, peace, contentment, and a reputation that safeguards your household in times of hardship. Be mindful of your impact on others' lives, for your friends will come to your aid in times of need, whether you're destitute or wealthy. Charity is the currency of your soul.

IV. Save with Prudence

Storms will inevitably arise, obscuring the sun and releasing thunderous torrents of rain. Lightning may set the Earth ablaze. To believe that every season will be smooth sailing is mere fantasy. Those unprepared beg for mercy when the storms rage, but not you. Prepare for the uncertainties that lie ahead. Set aside a portion of your abundance, for just as the wise ant stores grains for winter, so should you accumulate reserves for times of need. The disciplined saver navigates the tempests with resilience. Life's labyrinth is fraught with mystery, unpredictable and treacherous for those caught unawares. Once again, recall the ant. While summer still reigns, it diligently prepares for the harshness of winter. Winter follows the harvest, and so does spring follow the bitter cold of winter's grasp. Assess your bounty and set aside a tenth of all you possess. Invest it wisely— whether in silver, gold, land, or any other commodity of enduring value. With a well-stocked pantry and mature prudence, your sleep will be sound, and your days resilient.

V. Invest with Wisdom

Set aside a tenth of all your earnings and entrust it to seasoned merchants who possess an in-depth understanding of the nuances of trade. The fertile ground of opportunity yields bountiful harvests for those who sow seeds with discernment. Beware of the smooth talker and extravagant appearances, for they often ensnare the curious and lazy soul. Exercise prudence in your investments, for they are the seeds that may flourish into mighty trees of abundance or lead you into the depths like a startled hare. Never yield your fortune on a single recommendation; be cautious of those who promise extraordinary returns, as their intentions may be cunning and malevolent. Remain vigilant against the thief and the schemer, for they prey on the vulnerable and burdened. Study the lives of those who offer wealth-building services; discern between those who have enriched many and those who have deceived many. Stay true to your conscience and value yourself enough not to be beguiled by luxury or false promises. It is wiser to accumulate knowledge than to blindly trust merchants from distant lands with your wealth. Therefore, delve into the wisdom of the wealthy, the merchants, and the traders who have come before you. Recognize the passage of time and the incremental steps taken to amass fortunes. Above all, diversify your investments like a well-tended garden, allowing the fruits of prudence to multiply. Rapid wealth accumulation is often a curse. Seasons of sowing, nurturing, harvesting, preserving, and sharing build the resilience and character of those who seek wealth. Sudden riches are burdensome to those lacking understanding. All substantial achievements require time, and when time is disregarded in the pursuit of wealth, it swiftly becomes a thief, leading to inevitable loss. Without the virtue of patience, essential for reaping what is sown, wealth will vanish like mist in the grasp of a clenched fist.

VI. Guard Against Avarice

Beware the perilous path of insatiable desire. Let not the pursuit of wealth consume your very essence. Wealth in gold, spices, robes, and land does not define your essence; aspire instead to be measured by the eternal fruits of virtue – Love, Joy, Peace, Temperance, Kindness, Goodness, Faithfulness, Gentleness, and Self-Control. If you attain these treasures of truth and gather them as diligently as the dust of the earth, you will possess the truest wealth. As Epictetus once said, 'Wealth consists not in having great possessions, but in having few wants.'

Have you heard of Solomon's flowers? You should. The fields bloomed in full splendor under the sun, unashamed in the presence of even the finest robes worn by the king.

A trail marked by tears is a heavy price to pay for a lifetime of gold. A heart burdened by greed becomes a ship lost in turbulent seas, perpetually tossed by the waves, far from the safety of the shore. Prioritize service over acquisition and strive for peace. Discover contentment in having enough. Cherish the simple joys of life—the breath of air, the scent of a flower, the laughter of a child, the caw of a raven, the touch of rain, the embrace of sleep, the enigma of a dream, the sight of stars, the yearning for love, and the act of giving it. These treasures are priceless and everlasting. When held dear and protected, they outshine the allure of gold and silver, bowing in reverence to the true wealth found within. Ultimately, love reigns supreme as the purest form of wealth.

VII. Teach the Legacy

Pass down the sacred wisdom to future generations. Engrave these teachings into the annals of family history. Let the scroll of wealth wisdom become a cherished heirloom, a guiding light for descendants as they navigate the currents of prosperity. The legacy of wealth transcends mere gold; it resides in the enduring virtues it fosters. The virtues of the Temple of Wisdom and Truth endure beyond the material wealth perceived by man. Indeed, gather the riches of the earth, but steward them with care during your earthly tenure. For nothing earthly is redeemed when the Spirit of the Air calls forth your soul. Therefore, heed the wisdom of the ages—Sow, Reap, Give, Procreate, Teach, and Learn.

May these ancient teachings illuminate the tapestry of existence, guiding those who traverse its threads with grace and sagacity toward prosperity.

CHAPTER 6

EMBRACING THE VIRTUES

"The Sage of Havenbrook," they would exclaim, "You must seek his counsel, hear his words!" The itinerant merchants spread the message with fervent zeal, igniting curiosity far and wide.

From distant villages to bustling towns, from common folk to nobility and kings, all yearned for the profound teachings. Elwic's heartfelt tales of redemption illuminated the virtues of honesty, kindness, courage, humility, and integrity as essential pillars for a fulfilling existence. His consistent exhortation to embody these virtues in daily life resonated deeply. Elwic emphasized that a life guided by such principles fosters harmony within society, an eternal truth transcending time until the end of days.

"Ultimately, it boils down to the individual willing to shoulder responsibility for their thoughts, actions, and the ensuing consequences. One who comprehends internal self-governance transcends the need for external laws or moral codes. Such individuals excel at instructing others in external governance, enforcing the rule of law upon those incapable of self-regulation."

Preferring to err on the side of grace, Elwic imparted the

teaching that all inevitably fall short of the ideal, and unfortunately, many continue to punish themselves long after the debt has been paid.

"We extend forgiveness and love to those who admit their wrongdoing, yet we often hold ourselves in contempt. True justice lies in paying the price for our missteps once. Eternal shame holds no sway over those who have embraced forgiveness," he would counsel. His words stirred both comfort and conflict among his audience. While some grew resentful of his message, the majority found solace in it. Elwic refrained from judgment; instead, he encouraged his followers to examine their own hearts considering timeless wisdom and truth. Most concurred that Elwic served not as judge and jury, but rather as a catalyst for the conscience of their souls. In his teachings, absolute truth prevailed, regardless of the speaker.

The Sage of Havenbrook graciously offered wisdom and counsel to all who sought his guidance. Though the multitude of questions posed to him would eventually be recorded on scrolls for future reference—a tale to be recounted in another chapter, upon the arrival of Actar, his disciple.

Regarding the pursuit of balance, Elwic cautioned, "Do not strive for balance in every aspect of your life. You will harvest the fruits of the seeds you have sown. To be dismayed by the eventual outcome is folly. Instead, focus on excelling in what you do best. The rest will naturally fall into place, even if others must step in to compensate for your shortcomings. Acknowledge your faults and commend those who bolster your weaknesses. Yet, understand that achieving perfect balance is an endeavor you can never fully achieve."

Elwic emphasized the significance of grasping the delicate equilibrium between work and leisure, duty and personal fulfilment, and the material concerns that beset us juxtaposed with the spiritual aspirations we harbor.

"It is often preached that by finding balance across various domains, individuals can lead lives that are more enriching and virtuous. However, it is unrealistic to anticipate that every facet of life will be in perfect harmony, and indeed, the pursuit of such balance can become a burdensome task. Which one perceives as just and equitable in their own life may be entirely incongruous in another's. Instead of striving for an existence marked by fairness, as defined by external standards, devote yourself to nurturing the innate talents bestowed upon you, treating them as precious jewels. Resist the temptation to adopt another's vision for your life; rather, tend to the garden that sprouts from your own seeds. The essence of life's balance lies in discerning which tasks are meant for you and which are not. Liberating oneself from the weight of external expectations is the key to attaining the true equilibrium we all yearn for," Elwic would conclude with a sigh, leaving those who listened to wonder whether he was fatigued or troubled.

On the Practice of Self-Reflection: The Sage of Havenbrook would earnestly counsel seekers to embrace regular self-reflection. Delving into introspection, individuals can evaluate their thoughts, actions, and intentions, identifying areas for growth and aligning their conduct with virtuous principles. Self-reflection also fosters the development of self-awareness and empathy toward others—a trait seldom found in those who prioritize personal gratification over moral integrity.

"Do not elevate yourself above others," the Sage would admonish. "For in doing so, you risk falling beneath the very standards you disdain. And what then? Will your ego stand as a pedestal of pride, subject to mockery and derision from those who witness your fall? Or would humility elevate you, earning you honor as one who is unassuming and deserving of forgiveness?"

Ensure that a beating heart does not merely echo its own praises, but humbly seeks virtue.

On the Practice of Cultivating Empathy and Compassion:
Elwic emphasized the vital role of empathy and compassion in
leading a virtuous life. He urged seekers to empathize with
others, to walk in their shoes and understand their perspectives.
Elwic advocated treating all individuals with kindness and
understanding, dismantling the barriers and armor of self-
righteousness.

"No one can fully comprehend the journey another must
endure unless they walk alongside them or step into their
struggle. Ignorance and prejudice are inherent blinders that
obstruct our view. It's easy to overlook the uniqueness of one's
own path, blessed by inherited privilege, while others bear the
burdens imposed by their ancestors. In this world, some dwell
in fields of suffering, while others reside in palaces of luxury.
Some prosper through virtuous deeds, while others suffer under
the oppressive rule of tyrants. Some find favor by transcending
cultural boundaries, while others face the consequences of their
own misdeeds. Regardless of the lens through which we view
our fellow humans, we cannot fully grasp their history or
predict their future. Thus, it is wise to show compassion without
judgment, recognizing the limitations of our understanding.
Compassion extends not only to our fellow humans but also to
the entire natural world and all living beings. If one can mistreat
a fellow human, then surely, they are indifferent to the well-
being of the animal kingdom. Yet, the natural world sustains the
life and breath of every living creature—from the bee and the
ant to the algae in the sea. Therefore, let us cultivate empathy
and compassion, ensuring that our lives are marked by kindness
and understanding."

On the Practice of Fostering Knowledge and Wisdom: The
Sage of Havenbrook would instill in his followers the
importance of embracing lifelong learning and the pursuit of
wisdom. Elwic encouraged seekers to immerse themselves in
reading, contemplation, and meaningful discussions to broaden

their understanding of the world and gain more profound insights. By expanding their knowledge and applying wisdom to their actions, individuals can make more informed and virtuous choices.

"The inherent flaw of human nature lies in the tendency to elevate opinions to the status of truth or facts when, in reality, they are merely constructs of mortal minds," Elwic cautioned. "On the final reckoning day, all souls will be confronted with the one ultimate truth, and all will come to realize their fallibility. Not a single soul will be exalted as omniscient. Instead, all will be admonished for their inherent biases as members of humanity—a collective prone to arrogance and the desire for godlike recognition. The prideful fall of humanity will be corrected. The root sin of all misery lies in the unchecked ego."

On the Practice of Gratitude: Elwic often found himself shaking his head in disbelief as he observed the pervasive lack of gratitude among the townsfolk, despite his repeated teachings on the matter. Recognizing the stubbornness inherent in human nature, he continued to stress the importance of cultivating gratitude for life's blessings.

"Expressing gratitude," he would counsel, "nurtures a positive mindset, nudges humility to life, and opens our eyes to the wonders that surround us." By acknowledging the gifts, they have received and offering thanks to the Creator and those who have shown them love and kindness, seekers can create a cycle of giving and receiving.

"Gratitude possesses the remarkable ability to alter our perception of reality," Elwic would assert. "Our outlook on what is and what can be is profoundly influenced by our attitude of gratitude. I urge you to embrace this virtue wholeheartedly and allow it to infuse richness into your lives. Without it, existence becomes bleak, bitter, and bereft of joy."

The Sage of Havenbrook emphasized the importance of openly and sincerely expressing gratitude. He encouraged his followers to let those around them know how much they are appreciated and the positive impact they have on their lives. He regarded this practice as a simple exercise with profound and lasting effects.

According to his teachings, small acts of kindness create a sense of community, and thoughtfulness from one's neighbors inspires a spirit of gratitude. His words struck a chord, prompting those inclined toward love to be the first to put this into practice. Eventually, even those less inclined became recipients of gratitude, until reciprocity became a natural urge from within.

"My dear followers and students, let us embrace gratitude as a guiding virtue in our daily lives," Elwic would exhort with earnestness. "Even the smallest effort to acknowledge the good in each day can illuminate the darkness that once clouded our vision. Let us, therefore, cultivate a deep appreciation for the blessings we encounter and the people who enrich our existence. Through gratitude, we enhance our own well-being and nurture the relationships that bring us joy and peace. May you tread the path of gratitude with an open heart and a spirit overflowing with thankfulness. And let us remember, with humility, that all things shall find their rightful place, whether in life or in death. Therefore, let us be grateful for the opportunity to experience these blessings here and now."

On the Practice of Integrity: the Sage of Havenbrook emphasized its paramount importance in every aspect of life, whether it pertained to trade, the fulfilment of promises, the dispensation of justice, or the execution of fair deeds.

He counseled seekers to remain steadfast in their commitment to truthfulness, sincerity, and moral principles, even when no one is watching. "Upholding integrity", he explained, "not only earns the trust and respect of others but also ensures one remains aligned with their virtuous path."

"There is no greater disservice than making pledges of honor, promising to fulfill them, only to backtrack and claim ignorance of the agreement," he admonished. "It is essential to acknowledge one's fallibility and, when necessary, take ownership of one's actions and their consequences. This brings a profound peace to the heart, knowing that one has remained true to their word. Woe to the one who refuses the mantle of responsibility – though one may refuse to pay honor to the truth, fate pays homage to the ego that dismisses humility; a payment heavy and cumbersome to bear."

Elwic's voice rang with sincerity and conviction as he continued, "Integrity becomes a natural law governing both the will and the conscience, free from regret. It is the unwavering commitment to honesty, truthfulness, and consistency in one's words, actions, and values."

With unwavering candor, he stressed, "All creatures, regardless of stature, have the capacity for authenticity, even in their shortcomings. Strive to be a person of substance, not one plagued by the poverty of flawed character; a person of fortitude, not one hindered by cowardice or lethargy."

He urged listeners to value honesty, even when it requires sacrifice, for integrity of mind is a rare strength among mortals, capable of shining as a beacon amidst the shadows of depravity. "Be prepared to weather the arrows aimed at harming you as you stand firm in truth and wisdom," he declared. "Your word will be a bastion of reliability and strength, impervious to doubt or dissent, while others may falter under the weight of conformity. Let your word be as strong as iron and steel, imbued with unwavering power. None will reject the power of your promise. Uphold your name as a Tower of Stability and a Treaty of Strength, for it shall speak for you in times of need when you cannot advocate for yourself."

Elwic, the Sage of Havenbrook, imparted to his followers the vital importance of embodying integrity in a world often clouded by deceit and dishonesty. He urged them to uphold the highest standards of conduct, recognizing that their actions would send ripples outward, shaping the world around them.

Integrity, he emphasized, defines one's character and dictates their interactions with the world, requiring unwavering commitment, honesty, and consistency.

"Let us strive," he urged, "to embody integrity in every facet of our lives. By doing so, we cultivate trust, genuine authenticity, and pave the way for a brighter future for ourselves and those we touch. May the path of integrity lead us to a haven of truth and righteousness, transcending the limitations of mere human nature."

Acknowledging the inherent struggle, he added, "There exists a Spirit within us, calling us to purity, yet in our human frailty, we often fall short of that which is attainable. Therefore, let us seek and ask for that which seems impossible to achieve without divine intervention. Integrity remains elusive until the ego is humbled and surrendered."

Elwic's teachings, though profound and transformative, offered only a glimpse of the wisdom he imparted as the son of a humble carpenter. Like salt that awakens thirst, may his lessons continue to inspire and nourish the hearts of those who seek truth and wisdom on their journey.

Take a moment now, Student of the Sage, to reflect on these words inscribed by me, Actar, the scribe of Havenbrook.

CHAPTER 7

SIRION THE STEWARD

THE INHABITANTS OF HAVENBROOK BEGAN TO ROUSE AT THE FIRST crow of the rooster. Soon, the gentle tinkling of bells adorning Sirion's goats could be heard. His daily journey to the hills surrounding Havenbrook ensured his two companions had the first taste of the fresh morning dew on the grass. Sirion counted himself fortunate. The scarcity of goats, compared to the abundance of sheep herds, kept his business lucrative. His specialty milk and delicious cheese were rich with flavor, and much sought after by visiting dignitaries. Naturally, prices were raised during the summer months, coinciding with these visits. Yet, Sirion remained both shrewd and fair with the residents of Havenbrook; sustaining a year-round income was essential to his livelihood. "Ah," he gestured to the sky, "But there are those who can offer more than mere pence or two!" With a chuckle, he veered off the well-trodden dirt road and ascended toward the base of the hill.

"Sirion!" a voice called out.

Sirion turned to see a figure draped in robes, seemingly gliding toward him. It was Elwic, his dear friend and mentor. A broad smile adorned Sirion's face as Elwic approached, his jests already evident. "Dear Elwic, have you come to partake in the morning nectar with Ja and Neen?" Sirion had christened his goats after a passing lady merchant who had briefly stopped in Havenbrook during its transition from hamlet to village. Though she hadn't stayed to witness the town's growth, she had developed a fondness for goat cheese, despite finding the town too primitive for her wares to thrive. Their friendship, like so many others in Havenbrook, was fleeting.

She had chuckled at the names he'd chosen for his animals—Meek and Mo. "What shall I call them, then?" he had asked, hoping to alleviate her amusement. After a moment's thought, she had suggested naming them after herself, a suggestion that left Sirion momentarily speechless. Despite her small stature, her courage to traverse merchant trails signaled her strength, as did her laughter, which commanded attention. Occasionally, the glint of metal would catch the light as she moved, revealing her weapon of choice: a sharp knife! As was customary with newcomers in Havenbrook, wary eyes scrutinized her attire, searching for clues to her origins. However, her quick grasp of the local language and her genuine curiosity swiftly won over the townsfolk. Within hours, the baker, the tanner, the tea maker, and the sheep herder were all eager to embrace the sprite. Her sparkling eyes and sharp wit dispelled any lingering doubts about her intentions, leaving behind only warmth and acceptance.

Sirion admired her outspokenness but couldn't help shaking his head. "Naming a beast after a lady? Perhaps you've still got some bad ale lingering from the night before."

"Nay!" she protested. "I've only had your milk and a small gulp of ale to wash it down." She huffed, "I've got a name you can split in two, so each goat can have its own."

Sirion rubbed his chin thoughtfully. "You've been here a week, and I've never asked. What is your name?"

She met his gaze proudly, declaring, "JaNeen." She waited for her words to impress him, but his reaction was unremarkable; even when a fly landed on his cheek, he didn't flinch. "Did you not hear?" she asked, tilting her head to check if he had dozed off while standing. But Sirion remained motionless.

"Hey, Sirion! Did you hear the name, JaNeen? It's the best you can do for your two beasts!" She wasn't accustomed to being ignored. "Wake up, Goat Man! Ja and Neen! Don't you get it?"

Sirion continued to stare in silence. He had heard every word. JaNeen was unaware of his thoughts. He felt honored by her suggestion for Meek and Mo. The names he had chosen had originally been a jest at the expense of the gangly creatures he had raised since birth. But now, Ja and Neen! The name she offered, now split into two, seemed perfect and symbolic—as though a touch of royalty had been bestowed upon the smelly goats of Havenbrook.

Sirion was renowned for two things: the special milk and cheese he crafted from these seemingly obstinate creatures. And now, these beasts could ascend to the heights of nobility with the mere bestowal of a new name; a name befitting their esteemed status in the village. They produced a bounty of flavor, enriching the village through their mere existence. Why shouldn't they be honored? Sirion pondered, savoring the thought like a delectable treat, his mouth watering.

"Of course, I heard you. I am captivated by the gift of your name," Sirion said, turning away from the merchant of crafts. He crouched down, summoning his creatures, Meek and Mo, who eagerly approached their master. Sirion tenderly caressed their faces one by one, naming them in a simple yet meaningful ceremony.

"Today, you are Ja," he murmured, rubbing his cheek against Meek's jaw line. "And today, you are Neen," he repeated, bestowing the same affectionate gesture upon Mo. Rising to his feet, he gently patted their heads, making the proclamation official. Their joyous bleats seemed to echo the celebration of their newfound status among the beasts of Havenbrook.

"Yes, good names!" Sirion exclaimed, turning back to the lady merchant, who shone like a rare jewel amidst the tattered rags of travelers.

"Thank you," he said, bowing toward JaNeen with admiration and respect.

JaNeen smiled. "See! Now, you will remember me!"

The following morning, as Sirion released Ja and Neen from their pen, he couldn't help but scan the edge of the village where the traveling merchants parked their caravans. Despite it being just a week since she arrived and joined him on his morning walks, a strange sense of emptiness gripped his heart. One spot stood conspicuously vacant—the spot where JaNeen had camped and displayed her goods.

His heart sank. JaNeen had departed before dawn without a word of farewell. All Sirion had left of her was her name. Perhaps it was a parting gift, meant to ensure he remembered her. He recalled her words, "See! Now, you will remember me!" But he couldn't repay her gesture.

"I've come to speak with you," Elwic's voice cut through the fog of Sirion's thoughts. "I promise not to distract you or Ja and Neen," he added with a chuckle.

Sirion nodded. "It is my honor, dear Sage of Havenbrook. What is it you wish to discuss?"

"Ah, the questions, Sirion. I have questions for you!" Elwic gestured toward the ancient oak tree that stood sentinel over the village. "There, we shall speak. I have fond memories of discovering treasure at the roots of that tree, and today, I seek the treasure you hold hidden in your heart."

Sirion raised an eyebrow inquisitively. "My treasure? I possess only two goats and the skill of cheese-making!" He chuckled at his own words. "Apart from that, I live among the smelliest of creatures and have no family to pass on my craft." Pausing to reflect, he added, "The only treasure I have is the memory of a lady who named my goats!" Another chuckle escaped him.

"Oh, dear Sirion, you possess a treasure that many yearn for, and that treasure will only grow when put into practice," Elwic said, his smile gentle and his eyes full of love.

"What treasure do you speak of, of which I am unaware?" Sirion's voice trembled with curiosity.

"Let us climb the hill to the tree and sit awhile, and I will draw it out from you," Elwic's voice held a quiet strength that demanded attention.

Ja and Neen settled in, enjoying the succulent reeds of grass seasoned by the morning dew as their master ascended the hill with the sage toward the ancient oak tree.

"The grass is particularly tasty this morning," Elwic remarked, nodding toward the goats. "They are safe here, Sirion. Our time together is destined."

Sirion nodded, taking a moment to observe the tall grass swaying gently in the crisp breeze above the goats' short-haired backs. They were content, grazing in blissful ignorance. With a sigh, Sirion joined Elwic, who had settled at the base of the tree.

"I've summoned you here to discuss a virtue that holds great importance to me, one that connects us deeply to the very earth beneath our feet: stewardship," Elwic began, gesturing toward the village, the fields, and the distant forest. "We are mere custodians of this land, entrusted with its care for but a fleeting moment. Just as the sun rises and sets, so do we traverse this world, leaving behind a legacy."

Sirion's eyes met Elwic's with a mix of surprise and humility. "You, my friend, Sirion the cheesemaker, have been steadfast in your reverence for the land and the creatures under your care. I want you to understand that I have observed your actions, as have many in our town. Your virtuous stewardship of these hills is widely known. You, Sirion, are a guardian of the earth. Do you grasp the significance of your role?"

Sirion gasped at the honor bestowed upon him by the wise sage of Havenbrook. "I cannot fathom such praise!" He briefly glanced over his shoulder to check on his goats—contentedly chewing with closed eyes, basking in the warmth of the sun. "I simply do what my heart deems right. As for a calling of a higher purpose, I am unsure. My devotion lies with these cherished creatures." Sirion gestured toward his beloved goats. "If that constitutes a calling, then I am guilty of fulfilling it."

Elwic nodded, a gentle smile gracing his lips. "Your calling is stewardship. It goes beyond mere cultivation of fields or tending to livestock. It is a sacred obligation to ensure that our actions leave this land, and its bounty enriched for future generations." He paused, seeing Sirion fully engaged. "There exists a delicate equilibrium between taking and giving, between nurturing the earth so it may continue to provide for posterity. Sirion, you have embodied this principle for as long as I've known you. By rotating your goats to different pastures, allowing the grass to rejuvenate and flourish, you transcend selfishness and indolence. In this act of stewardship, the healthful grass they consume is transformed into milk, and through your conscientious efforts, into cheese. Do you see? The quiet treasure within you expresses itself loudly. You are Sirion the Steward!"

Sirion felt tears welling in his eyes, his lips trembling, and his chest heaving with the deepest breath of cleansing he had ever experienced.

Elwic's voice resonated with thunderous power, commanding the surrounding wind to bow in deference, seeking refuge in anonymity. The authority of his words was undeniable, humbling even the mightiest of beings.

"Sirion. Hear my words." Elwic's voice rang out. "You have not depleted the land of its vitality; instead, you have nurtured it with love, allowing it to flourish and provide for you in return. The streams that quench your thirst, you have kept pure. Even the morning dew is left untouched, a gift for other creatures to enjoy. Look." Elwic pointed to a timid deer on a hill opposite the town road. "That deer may not have these fields to graze upon if not for your daily stewardship."

Sirion was rendered speechless, his throat tight with emotion at the praise that had touched both his ears and his soul.

"And so tonight, Sirion, I am teaching about you, about your acts of kindness toward the earth and the enduring impact they have for generations to come."

Hours passed, and true to his word, Elwic expounded upon the principles of stewardship. The fire crackled, casting flickering shadows upon the rocks. The people of Havenbrook listened intently as Elwic concluded his discourse on stewardship, bestowing upon Sirion the title of "Sirion the Steward," the guest of honor.

Sirion was not only deserving of praise but also held up as an exemplar, a beacon of virtue to inspire others in the practice of stewardship.

"Remember," Elwic proclaimed, "true stewardship is not a burden but a privilege. It is a harmonious dance with nature, a partnership with the essence of life itself. Embrace this virtue, and you shall find your lives enriched in ways beyond imagination." Pointing toward Sirion, Elwic urged the townsfolk to applaud the lifelong dedication of their honored guest. Sirion, humbled by the recognition, realized that his wisdom had sown seeds that, with diligent care, had grown into a mighty tree, its roots entwined with the very soul of Havenbrook. With a bowed head, he shed tears of gratitude. His life, once seemingly modest with only two goats by his side, held newfound significance.

That night, an ancient dance was rekindled; the dance of stewardship that all who took it seriously learned the steps to build a stronger future. And from that day forth, the fields flourished, yielding even more bountiful crops. The forest, content with their guardianship, provided vibrant protection, and the people lived with purpose and passion, embracing the ethos of living within their means.

CHAPTER 8

THE PERIL OF THE UNPREPARED

The chill of late autumn sent brisk breezes through the narrow cobblestone street of Havenbrook. Anika, the tea maker, huddled under a woolen blanket by the front door of her shop, savoring a brew of lilac and mint. "Whew," she exhaled, blowing the top layer of heat away from her clay mug. "Every year without fail..." Her thoughts trailed off as she shook her head.

The "rickety-rack-rack" of a wagon pulled by a wayfaring stranger in town was not a welcome sight. It signaled an unprepared merchant who had failed to consider the changing seasons, trade routes, and the distance between towns as autumn began to give way to winter's slumber.

"The world is veiled in shadows of ignorance, and as long as mankind draws breath, we must continually teach the same truths," Anika mused, reflecting on the cyclical nature of wisdom. "The darkness is feeble, and light casts no shadow. Embrace the light and face each hour and each day with a hope that darkness cannot comprehend. Store the oil and the wick, and your house will be blessed with peace. By preparing for the storm, even if your feast is plain, your belly will be full, and your rest assured. Go, set aside enough for the season and an extra tenth besides."

The words of Elwic's teachings on the virtues of prudence and preparedness echoed in Anika's mind, reminding her of the importance of foresight and readiness in the face of life's uncertainties.

He recited the ancient text, "Observe the ants and learn from their ways. Even amid summer, they diligently prepare for winter. While mortality is inevitable, one's life can endure as a legacy. There will come a time when others hunger for sustenance, and your words will nourish their souls like bread. Though the mortal body may wither, inner renewal is possible. Therefore, do not allow idleness to approach your doorstep, yet be cautious of its allure; for the spirit of sloth may linger unreasonably. Even when there is need, the emergence of your talent may be perceived as an affront to their recovery. Provide for the needy but be mindful of the offspring you bring forth."

Anika mused to herself, "Even a squirrel stores acorns before the snow arrives. Yet, here wanders this solitary merchant, disregarding the seasonal rhythms." She shook her head, attempting to resist the impulse to open the door. But her resolve faltered, and she succumbed to curiosity.

"Are you lost, lad, or do you court danger as winter draws near?" Her words slipped out before she could stop them, and she regretted their sharpness instantly.

The merchant turned his gaze toward the tea shop, examining the sign above the door, adorned with a banner symbolizing hospitality.

"Oh, my lady! Your words are a balm to my weary soul. A warm drink and perhaps a loaf of bread would be a welcome gift to this traveler, if you would be so kind," he appealed.

Anika couldn't help but note his cunning nature. "I shall offer you tea in your own cup, but what have you to offer in return?" she inquired, her tone wary.

The pilgrim's expression soured slightly. His notion of hospitality seemed limited to receiving rather than engaging in a fair exchange.

With a deliberate gesture, he stooped to adjust the handles of his cart, the sound of wood scraping against stone filling the air momentarily before he straightened up. Then, with a theatrical flourish, he turned around as if about to unveil a miraculous elixir. "Behold, my lady, the marvels of my merchandise are deserving of your patronage." He smiled, black spaces were caves where teeth once graced.

Anika suppressed an eye roll. "A poet and a jester, it seems," she thought to herself, deciding to keep her opinions to herself.

He scoured the ground with fervor, his movements akin to a foraging animal, until he abruptly halted, lifting his head with a slightly awkward tilt, his eyes widening in a manner reminiscent of an owl.

"Oh heavens! This is beyond compare!" he exclaimed, swiftly concealing his discovery with the finesse of a practiced salesman – presenting a treasure only to retract it with a calculated flourish.

"What was that?" Anika interjected; her frustration was evident. "Oh no, he's deceived me", she whispered, her thoughts leaked betraying her assessment of his cunning nature.

The merchant stole a glance toward Anika before carefully retrieving the gem he had feigned burying. "Ah, this?" he pivoted, revealing a dark blue glass bottle of irregular shape. "This is the craftsmanship of an artisan I encountered in a city – yes, a city, unlike..." he surveyed his surroundings dismissively, "unlike this place."

His voice dripped with disdain but Anika retorted. "This 'place' is my hamlet, my home, my village – now, according to the cartographers, a town. I assure you; it deserves as much respect as any other," Anika bristled at the traveler's condescending tone, branding him a rogue in her mind.

"Oh, my lady! I harbor no ill will towards he paused, feigning forgetfulness, "What was it you called it?"

Anika seethed with indignation. Initially poised to storm into her shop and slam the door shut, she reminded herself of the importance of reserving judgment until all evidence was presented.

Inhaling deeply, she composed herself. "Havenbrook," she pronounced firmly, her lips forming the "k" with emphasis. "Havenbrook" is the name of this town. Have you not heard of it?"

"I am called Randolf. I am familiar with Havenbrook, though I confess, I was unaware of my arrival here. But now, I am enlightened," he replied, attempting to convey contrition with a shrug. Anika saw through his facade, perceiving his apology as disingenuous.

"Randolf, you may masquerade as a merchant, but I find 'jester' to be a more fitting title. Randolf the Jester!" she quipped, unable to resist the jab.

Randolf recoiled, his eyes widening, his chest swelling with protest. "Please, if you knew the caliber of individuals who count me as a friend, you would retract that epithet."

"Oh! Then it shall be Randolf the non-Jester?" Anika prodded further. "You are NOT what you seem." She smirked. "And as for that blue bottle, it's a reject from a glassmaker in the neighboring town. I know him well; he's discarded many such pieces. You've merely salvaged one and are attempting now to pass it off as valuable."

Randolf was visibly disconcerted, his facade crumbling as he was exposed as a peddler of inferior goods. Eager to salvage what remained of his reputation, he hurriedly reached for the handles of his cart, intending to depart before the town caught wind of his deceit. But just as he bent over, ready to make his escape...

"Wait!" Anika's heart softened with compassion. "I can offer you a warm drink, but I've no bread to spare. My trade for bread with my tea is reserved for every third day."

Randolf straightened, observing Anika's departure, before she added, "Get your cup ready."

Moments later, Anika returned with a steaming cup of tea poured into a hollowed-out bone, the most rudimentary of vessels. "Thank you, tea-maker. Might I inquire about the whereabouts of the bread-maker?" Randolf asked.

Anika chuckled. "He's busy baking. Can't you smell it?" She gestured with her head. "If you have a nose, you'll find your way." With that, she absolved herself of any further obligation to the merchant, confident that the townsfolk would soon uncover his true nature. She chuckled at the rhythmic sound of his departure: rickety-rack-rack – rickety-rack-rack.

The day proved shorter than Randolf had anticipated. With nightfall approaching and not a single sale made, he found himself unprepared for the biting cold of dawn. The kiss of winter touched his cheeks. His attempts to attract customers fell flat, his wagon still burdened with unsold wares. The cheap goods he scavenged were now more of a hindrance than a boon. As the temperature dropped, the prospect of a harsh winter's night loomed. "Where shall I find rest? With no profits for ale, begging seems my only option," he muttered, his resolve wavering.

He pivoted on his heels, redirecting his steps toward the nearest shop when a flicker of light caught his eye. In the distance, a sizable fire blazed, offering a beckoning warmth against the icy taunts of the night. He recognized the folly of his defiance against the season's harsh bite, yet he dared to hope for leniency, as if mercy could be won through mere pleading. A scoundrel, he branded himself, aware of his own weaknesses and the sorrow born of neglecting the discipline he should have embraced long ago. Instead of laying the groundwork for security in his later years, he had drifted amidst lofty aspirations, neglecting the practicalities of saving, investing, and giving. Now, those neglected lessons loomed over him like mocking specters, haunting his dreams and tormenting his waking thoughts.

In his darkest nightmares, a massive black crow would swoop down, tearing threads from his tunic with each pass. Soon, other winged creatures joined the fray, stripping him bare until he knelt, hands clutching his throat in a futile attempt to protect himself. Blood seeped from the wounds inflicted by his avian assailants, staining the earth below as he lay defeated by the relentless march of time and his own stubborn pride. He knew the path he should have taken, but the opportunities for "should haves" had vanished, slipping away like sand through his fingers. Life ebbed away, draining with the fading light of day, leaving him desperate for sustenance, for any morsel of food to quell the gnawing hunger within. Stripped bare of hope, he was laid bare to the voice that pierced through the darkness.

"Follow me," came the command from the figure shrouded in darkness, their features obscured by the flickering light of the fire.

"I will indeed," Randolf accepted the stranger's invitation eagerly. "But pray, what is happening?"

The figure continued to stride forward, offering no response to Randolf's inquiries. As the dawn's light yeilded to the darkness of the sky, attention shifted to the animated shadows cast by the joyful movements of the gathered townsfolk. The murmurs of the crowd faded into the background as the mysterious figure glided through, taking his place of honor upon a makeshift podium fashioned from the base of a sturdy tree trunk. With the raise of his arms, silence fell over the assembly. His face remained hidden beneath the hooded cloak, veiling his eyes from view, yet exuding an aura of authority that captivated Randolf's attention.

This enigmatic figure simply was – no pompous introduction, no grand entrance. His presence cut through the throng of unwashed villagers and aimless wanderers, drawing them all into a solemn hush, punctuated only by the crackling of the bonfire.

As Elwic drew in a deep breath, preparing to address the gathered crowd, the soft crackle of burning wood seemed to defer to the weight of his impending words.

Elwic, the esteemed Sage of Havenbrook, raised both hands in perfect synchrony, delicately pulling back the veil that concealed the countenance of a revered teacher. A hushed gasp rippled through a portion of the crowd – these were the ones who had journeyed to Havenbrook in hopes of glimpsing the renowned master. Some were astonished at his plain appearance; others were disappointed that he did not shine as an angel would. He was mortal and just like them.

"My friends, behold the beauty of this fire," Elwic proclaimed, directing their attention to the flickering flames. "It warms us on this chilly night and imparts a valuable lesson."

Several visitors leaned in; their ears attuned to the wisdom about to be imparted.

"What is a fire if not an earnest testament to effort?" Elwic addressed the assembled faces. "Some among you demand heat from the fire without understanding the labor that precedes it. You scream, 'Give me heat' and yet fail to furnish what is needed before a harvest. You must first harvest the wood, allow it to season, and then, when the cold arrives, you fuel the stove. This fire we see before us did not ignite tonight; it was born many seasons ago. A tree was felled, cured, and stored until its energy could manifest as the warmth we now enjoy."

Elwic's gaze shifted to the traveling merchant. "You see, without foresight, one is destined for failure. Or, as the ancient book gives us fair warning – without a vision, the people perish."

Nods rippled through the crowd like ripples on a tranquil lake, echoing their agreement. The dancing shadows seemed to rejoice in the wisdom being shared, while the firelight danced upon toothless smiles.

A quavering voice pierced the murmurs, rising above the crowd with a plea. "Dear Sir, I implore you to address my plight." A hush fell over the gathering. "What about me? I have made no preparations for winter or the seasons to come. Is there hope for one such as I?"

The townsfolk transformed into silent spectators, forming a distinct barrier around the hesitant voice. A palpable awkwardness enveloped the merchant – the very same individual whom Anika had dismissed, the same soul who had reaped no profit that day, the same figure that now followed the cloaked Sage into the shadows at his beckoning, "Follow me."

Elwic let out a weary sigh, knowing that his response would pose a formidable challenge for the weary petitioner. It would be words – words that illuminate the darkest recesses of the heart, words that confront past decisions, words that demand introspection and accountability.

"Tonight, you are offered shelter and sustenance, a gesture of compassion bestowed upon you. Consider it grace," Elwic began, his voice carrying the weight of wisdom. "As for your future, that path lies within your own hands. Your question reveals an awareness of the seeds of opportunity you may have squandered in life's early days. Yet, even in your smallest blessings – the breath in your lungs, the sight of majestic mountains, the touch of the earth beneath your feet, the scent of a delicate flower, the taste of humble bread – there lies solace. These are privileges denied to the departed; if they had a wish to live, your meager presence could be their feast, but they have no choice. As the ancient philosopher Plato once remarked, 'Only the dead know the end of war.' Rest assured; you speak with a truth I bear witness to. Tonight, find peace within the tower I have erected for you. And on the morrow, carry forward with the life that remains. Let the weight of past regrets and the bounty of present blessings guide your steps toward a future of redemption."

It was late, the evening chill nipping at the edges of the ring of fire, teasing the backs of the townsfolk. They turned as one towards their cozy homes, the lesson concluded, and those who had gleaned its wisdom nodded in solemn understanding. The outsider garnered pity, but only for the night. Within the tower, he would find solace in a roasted potato, a cup of ale, and a fleeting respite before the inevitable reckoning of the next day. His heaven was but a fleeting reprieve from the impending hell of the morrow.

As dawn broke, a wispy breath escaped his lips, lingering briefly before dissipating into the frosty air. He turned to find a cart to his left, a hill to his right, its slope leading up to a line of trees that seemed to silently rebuke him for his shortcomings.

With a start, the merchant sat upright, only to discover that the town of Havenbrook had vanished, leaving him stranded and alone. The path ahead and the path behind lay blanketed in snow, a stark reminder of his unpreparedness for the final season of the year and, perhaps, the final season of his life.

Anika busied herself pouring steaming water into a cup, her thoughts lingering on the stranger – the "jester" who had stumbled into Havenbrook a month prior, just as early winter had begun to settle in. He had stayed for but a day and a night, partaking in her tea, a meal, and a warm bed in the tower before departing the following morning. Despite the sage's teachings that fateful night, his heart remained untouched. His heart was cold, as cold as the winter that swallowed the season.

His lifeless body was discovered, frozen beneath a hill, nestled amidst a line of trees, blanketed by snow. He had not made himself ready for the ultimate season of the year nor for the final season of his own life.

Take a moment now, Student of the Sage, to reflect on these words inscribed by me, Actar, the scribe of Havenbrook. Pause now and receive the lesson.

CHAPTER 9

THE QUEST FOR THE ENCHANTED SCROLL

ELWIC WAS RENOWNED FOR HIS VAST KNOWLEDGE AND GENTLE wisdom, drawing inexperienced youths from distant lands who sought his counsel.

One day, a young and eager apprentice named Talib approached Elwic, his eyes brimming with curiosity. "Master Elwic," Talib began, "how does one acquire wisdom in a world so vast and mysterious? Would it be possible to attain the breadth of knowledge that you possess?"

Elwic's smile reflected the earnestness in Talib's gaze. Choosing to impart his wisdom through a parable, Elwic embarked on a tale crafted to illuminate the path to enlightenment. Though aware that only a fraction of his students would heed his words and act upon his teachings, Elwic humbly offered his lessons without reservation.

"Long ago, in a distant realm, there existed a hidden library guarded by a wise and ancient owl. This was the fabled Library of Knowledge," Elwic began. "Within its hallowed halls rested a single, enchanted scroll bearing a sacred inscription – 'Wisdom.' It was said to hold the key to truth and enlightenment, with the power to grant understanding of the very essence of life itself. Legends spoke of its ability to bestow untold wealth upon its reader. The manuscript was a compilation of sacred words, imbued with the wisdom of sages from across the ages. While its existence was shrouded in mystery, many dared to seek out the library, despite warnings from learned scholars who dismissed it as mere fantasy; they scoffed and scolded any seeker who deemed it worthy of strength and the breath to speak of it. 'Ha!' they would say, 'The discovery of this scroll, likened to a whisper in a dream. It's a fable and nothing more!'

Many a seeker embarked on perilous journeys in pursuit of this sacred place, yet few returned, and none claimed the coveted prize," Elwic reminisced, reflecting on his own quest to find the Temple of Wisdom and Truth. "Only those who search with the pure heart of a child, the protective instinct of a mother bear, and the unwavering determination of a lion defending its pride can endure the greatest trials in the pursuit of truth."

Talib listened attentively, his imagination ablaze with possibility.

"The first seeker was a knight adorned in gleaming armor, convinced that strength and valor alone would grant him the knowledge he sought. He charged through dense forests, heedless of the delicate balance of nature, trampling the underbrush as if it were an enemy of the realm. He battled fierce creatures; the squirrels and fawn barely escaped his wrath. Furthermore, he scoffed at the creatures of the woods, seeing them only as obstacles to be vanquished. Treacherous rivers were crossed with little regard for their significance. Yet, in his reckless haste, he failed to heed the whispered wisdom of the natural world – the rustling leaves, the secrets carried by the wind, the silent counsel of the ancient trees. His ego forbade humility to travel with him as a companion.

Arriving at the library, his heart was hollow, for he had overlooked the antiquities of wisdom that surrounded him. His quest had been driven by egotistical fantasies, his mind filled with visions of grandeur and glory.

The knight pranced his words to the wind. 'Songs will be sung of my exploits! My triumphs will echo through the ages! I am the Conqueror of the Hidden Library!' His vanity whispered words in his mind but quickly melted under the light of the everlasting sun; burned off just as the impurity of dross is to gold.

He discovered naught but his own reflection – for he sought not wisdom, but rather sought to glorify his own name, and in his vanity, found naught of true worth. He departed with less than he had come.

Talib contemplated the knight's journey and the sobering lesson it conveyed. One who pursues glory solely for the sake of glory shall find a sorrow that is not fit to be shared nor proclaimed.

"As for the second seeker," Elwic continued, "he was a learned scholar, steeped in the lore of books and parchments. He believed that knowledge alone would guide him to the elusive scroll. He immersed himself in ancient texts, unraveled cryptic codes, and deciphered forgotten languages. Meanwhile, his wife of many years fell ill with a fever, a result of a cut on her arm sustained while tending to the crops – a task that had been his own duty, yet he had shirked it onto her shoulders. His solution to her ailment was to send her away – viewing her as a nuisance, despite being the sole caretaker of their hungry children. A man obstinate in his ways, he treated his spouse, who had borne his lineage, with callous indifference. He showed little regard for the fellow humans who crossed his path, his disdain evident in the disdainful glances and contemptuous sighs he directed toward them. His lofty self-regard was tarnished by his relentless pursuit of the Hidden Library and the fabled scroll that promised to validate his superiority – allowing him to declare, I alone have unraveled the mysteries, and I alone possess the wisdom." Elwic leaned forward and sighed before he continued.

"However, in his singular focus on the written word, he turned a blind eye to the living world outside. His wife suffered a lonely and agonizing death, neglected in her time of need. The children, whom he barely acknowledged, found themselves destitute in a desolate and unforgiving landscape of poverty, preyed upon by unscrupulous individuals who exploited their vulnerable circumstances. He cursed the notion of familial legacy, damned by his own neglect.

Arriving at the library, his mind was cluttered with academic pursuits, devoid of the wisdom found in the vibrant tapestry of life. His thoughts were trapped within the musty confines of two-dimensional pages, while the richness of human connection and the warmth of familial love eluded him. The second seeker had been foolish, squandering a wealth of love and companionship for the fleeting promise of knowledge. His wife and children were his true treasures, yet he had cast them aside in pursuit of an illusory dream.

The riches he sought were within his grasp all along, in the simple joys of daily affection and familial bonds. The kiss from a child, the embrace of a spouse, the enchantment of a late-night story by the fire, or the warmth of an early morning gathering with children nestled close – these were the true treasures he traded away for a mere fraction of their worth, only to realize his loss in the end."

Talib absorbed the message, recognizing that wisdom transcended the confines of books and that family was a treasure beyond measure. As if attuned to his thoughts, Elwic awaited Talib's consent to continue. With a nod and a smile, Talib urged him forward.

"The third seeker," Elwic resumed, "was a humble gardener, attuned to the rhythms of nature, the dance of the seasons, and the delicate balance of chance. He nurtured his plants with tenderness and listened to the melodies of birds with reverence. To him, each dawn heralded a new beginning, a fresh canvas upon which life's beauty could unfold. His connection to the natural world filled his soul with wonder and awe."

He wandered through meadows and forests, inhaling the fragrance of blooming flowers and feeling the earth beneath his feet, finding solace in the resonance it brought him. Moving at a leisurely pace, he observed the dance of life unfolding around him. When he finally reached the library, his heart overflowed with contentment, for he had gleaned wisdom from the world around him. Even before arriving, he was fulfilled, grateful for the treasure of life itself. His riches lay in the froth of babbling waters, the vivid hues of nature, the tantalizing scents that caressed his senses, the gentle touch upon his skin, and the melodic sounds that soothed his spirit."

Elwic inclined his head toward Talib, maintaining a steady gaze. "Success, Talib, is not merely found at the culmination of a journey. It resides in the conquest, the struggle, and the very path we tread. Along every path lie challenges, trials, and moments of respite. Each serves a purpose and warrants respect for its existence."

Talib marveled at the gardener's journey, recognizing that wisdom could be gleaned from the simplest of moments. Of the three seekers, he found his heart drawn to the gardener. While he could admire the strength of the knight and appreciate the scholarly pursuits of the second seeker, it was the gardener who nourished his heart, mind, and soul. "That shall be my path!" Talib declared.

"Remember, Talib," Elwic gently reminded, "wisdom transcends the confines of books and battles. It is woven from the fabric of observation, reflection, and reverence for the world around us. Seek not only in grand quests or academic endeavors, but in the quiet whispers of nature and the wisdom of everyday life." With a slow nod and a raised eyebrow, Elwic signaled the end of the lesson.

Talib parted ways with Elwic, his spirit ignited with a newfound sense of purpose, ready to embark on his personal quest for wisdom. He pledged to approach each moment with the keen observation of the gardener, the profound reflection of the scholar, and the unwavering resolve of the knight.

As he bid farewell to Elwic, Talib bowed in gratitude, feeling a surge of determination coursing through him. With a resolute stride, he exited the tower, his resolve stronger than ever. Venturing into the world, he carried with him the parable of the enchanted scroll, a story that would serve as his guiding light on the journey ahead. It reminded him that true enlightenment transcended the confines of mere literature, scattered like precious gems across the vast expanse of existence, awaiting discovery by those with open hearts and eager minds.

And indeed, Talib's path eventually did lead him to the fabled Hidden Library and the Enchanted Scroll. With a pure heart as his key, he unlocked the gates and delved into the wisdom contained within. The truths inscribed upon the scroll became etched into his very being - a quill with eternal ink feathered the golden words on the tablet of his heart.

Before long, his name echoed throughout the land as "Talib the Traveler, the Bearer of the Enchanted Scroll", spreading enlightenment wherever he roamed. He asked and he received. He knocked and the doors were opened. He sought and he found the Spirit of Truth.

CHAPTER 10

HARMONY OF THE FIELDS

"O WISE SAGE OF HAVENBROOK! WHILE SOME LIVE IN OPULENCE, I scrape potatoes from the earth to sustain me. It seems unjust that I should be impoverished while others possess riches," lamented the villager.

The sage nodded, acknowledging the grievance, and began his response with a familiar tale:

"In the land of Eldoria, there dwelled a baron named Lord Aleron, overseeing the town of Prosper. Lord Aleron was known for his wisdom and fairness, he generously allowed peasants and cottars to cultivate the land for their livelihoods, reaping abundance in return. His outward prosperity mirrored the richness of his benevolent heart. As within, so without."

The audience gathered around the fire, eagerly awaiting the sage's narrative.

"Tomas, a humble cottar on the outskirts of Prosper, eked out a meager existence from his small plot of land. His sustenance consisted of simple fare: caudle for breakfast; the heated milk from his only goat brought warmth to his belly, and horse bread made from beans and legumes. Yet, he found solace in the earthy taste of his childhood sustenance." The crowd nodded in agreement, for they understood the taste of the earth. He continued.

"The prospect of Lord Aleron conversing with Tomas seemed as unlikely as a bear sharing pottage with a fish in the river. Yet fate intervened, bringing them together outside the tax hall of Eldoria.

And so it was, on that fateful day, Lord Aleron encountered Tomas tending his modest trellis of vegetables. The rickety fence made of twisted branches and vines brought a humorous smile to Aleron's face.

Despite the stark contrast in their stations, Aleron approached Tomas with genuine curiosity. He brought his horse to a stop and cleared his throat.

'Cottar,' he began, 'What is your given name?'

Tomas had heard the distant gallop, likening it to the routine rounds of a tax collector, but he dismissed any apprehension, knowing his dues were fully settled. He kept his focus on the trellis, muttering to himself, 'What does the tax man want? I owe nothing to your schemes!' He maintained his gaze, refusing to acknowledge the man behind the interruption.

Lord Aleron, unruffled by the brash retort, cleared his throat once more. 'Cottar, it is I, Lord Aleron, Baron of Eldoria, seeking your audience.'

Tomas's eyes widened in recognition. No man would falsely claim the name of Lord Aleron from atop a horse. A sudden chill of fear gripped him, traveling from his stomach to his head and down his back. Before he could respond, the menacing image of a sword piercing his innards flashed in his mind, paralyzing him with dread.

'Cottar! Turn and face me. I wish to know the name of the man to whom I am speaking', commanded Lord Aleron."

Elwic paused to survey his students. They listened with bated breath. He continued his tale.

"Slowly, Tomas turned, feeling an instinctual urge to prostrate himself before the nobleman. The phrase, 'the man to whom I am speaking,' echoed in his mind, acknowledging him as a man worthy of conversation, not mere chattel. He marveled at the sight before him—a Stoic figure atop a horse draped in royal purple, a stark contrast to his humble surroundings.

'My name is Tomas, esteemed Lord Aleron. Your presence honors me. How may I be of service?' Tomas responded with deference, bowing to show his respect.

Lord Aleron dismounted, offering a warm smile to Tomas. 'You may not have been aware of my customary visits to the fields of Eldoria. Typically, I stick close to the acres that yield our kingdom's grain, corn, and wheat.' He gestured toward the trellis. 'However, today, I've made an exception. I've heard of the struggles faced by cottars like yourself. Do you barely manage to feed yourself, or do you resort to pilfering from the fields to stave off hunger?'

Tomas momentarily regretted his proximity to his patch but quickly composed himself. 'I do not steal, Lord. Though my harvest is meager, I find solace in the honesty of my labor and for that, my soul prospers. Are you accusing me or simply testing my resolve with your words?'

Lord Aleron nodded approvingly. 'Ah, a man of honor, just as I had hoped. Your unwavering conviction speaks volumes of your character, not to mention your integrity.' He stepped forward, extending his hand for a shake. Seeing Tomas's hesitation, he chuckled. 'Fear not, my hand carries no poison.'

Reluctantly, Tomas shook his hand and, in doing so, touched his flesh, unaware that this simple gesture marked the beginning of a deeper bond of trust.

'I have a proposition for you,' Lord Aleron continued. 'Or rather, I would like to propose a collaborative arrangement that could benefit us both.'

Intrigued, Tomas nodded. 'Please, proceed.'

'You are a diligent and honest worker of the fields,' Aleron began. 'But observe me.' He glanced down at his attire with a hint of self-deprecation. 'I may have the finest clothing and cuisine in the kingdom, as did my father before me. However, what I lack is your expertise. I lack your patience, your wisdom in navigating the seasons' strengths and weaknesses.'

Tomas was taken aback by Aleron's humility, even in private conversation. 'What is it that you ask of me? What could a humble cottar like me offer a man of your stature?'

Lord Aleron took a deep breath, contemplating his proposal before finally speaking. 'I want you to tend to a neglected field of mine. It lies abandoned and overgrown, yet it holds the potential for great productivity with the right care. I need assistance, and in return, I offer you fair compensation along with a share of the harvest.'

Tomas's eyes widened in disbelief. 'You're offering me land without rent?'

'Exactly,' Lord Aleron confirmed. 'You will serve as my bailiff, cultivating the land with my resources—beasts, tools, and shelter—while I provide protection from hunger and taxes. Your labor will benefit my estate, and in turn, I will ensure your well-being.' He paused and rephrased his offer, 'I will provide the means for your labor, and you will provide the labor for my means.'

"Both men nodded in agreement." Elwic clapped his hands to break the spell. The captive audience woke with applause.

"This unlikely partnership flourished, proving advantageous for both parties. Tomas enjoyed security and sustenance, while Lord Aleron's wealth multiplied as he expanded his landholdings, providing similar opportunities to other peasants and cottars in need. Some of the bailiffs, inspired by Aleron's teachings, eventually purchased the lands they once tended, elevating themselves from humble beginnings.

Tomas, among the first to grasp the lessons of prosperity, applied Lord Aleron's counsel: 'Seek the commodity in short supply, and invest a tenth of all you have with the traders of that cause.' With diligence and foresight, Tomas transformed from a mere bailiff to a prosperous Franklin—a peasant turned wealthy landowner." Elwic looked about to survey the faces of his audience. He nodded as he saw the rapt attention to the story. He continued.

"Their collaboration sparked unprecedented prosperity, inspiring neighboring cottars to seek similar partnerships with their lords. Despite murmurs of jealousy and resentment among rival barons, evidence of the positive impact on the kingdom's economy silenced dissent. Crops flourished, hunger waned, wealth spread, and tax revenues soared, ushering in an era of shared prosperity through mutual business ventures.

Lord Aleron and Tomas passed down their legacy to their children, instilling a tradition of collaboration and mutual prosperity. And thus, my tale draws to a close. Are there any questions?"

One listener spoke up, voicing a sense of discontent. "I have not been fortunate enough to witness such prosperity in my own fields."

Elwic addressed the speaker directly. "Until you release your bitterness, your heart will remain closed to the possibility of new opportunities. You seek a gift rather than a trade. Your spirit erects barriers to growth. Beware the thief of jealousy, for it stifles the birth of ideas, stifles growth, and stifles the potential for your own legacy." A stillness settled in, yet for a second until he spoke again.

"I urge you to exchange your skills for silver and use a portion to sow seeds into the vast expanse of life. While some hoard their wealth selfishly, your concern is not with them. Your duty is to wisely utilize what you have, ensuring that the tree of your future begins with a seed. If you fail to plant, nurture, and feed your crop, you cannot blame those who do. Understand this: the rich offer opportunities to the poor. Those who seize them are rewarded, while those who do not - lament their ignorance. There will always be those who fail to comprehend the wealth available to them—aid the poor when you can, feed and clothe them, but do not attribute their plight solely to culture. Instead, teach them as I have taught you. For some, adherence to rules and guidance will lead to success, while others may find themselves in their current station in life as a result of their own actions.

Now, it is your responsibility to begin sowing into the soil of life. Wealth is earned, not bestowed. Foolishness squanders opportunities, but diligence yields abundance. Be generous even when impoverished, for it is through generosity that true richness is attained. These are the teachings passed down from ancient sages, the wisdom of Magister. I am but a humble vessel, a mere worm beneath the earth of their knowledge."

The people of Havenbrook fell silent, moved by Elwic's profound words. Some wept under the weight of his wisdom and humility. Though his words might have offended some, he spoke without reservation.

The one who had posed the initial question bowed his head in reflection, acknowledging his failure to take responsibility for his own actions and their consequences. The story of Tomas the Cottar and Lord Aleron served as a sobering reminder of his own shortcomings. He was eager to shed the cloak of victimhood and embrace accountability for his own fate.

Take a moment now, Student of the Sage, to reflect on these words inscribed by me, Actar, the scribe of Havenbrook.

CHAPTER II

HEATH THE TANNER

IN THE QUAINT MEDIEVAL VILLAGE OF THORNBRIDGE, NESTLED amidst rolling hills and dense forests, resided a tanner named Heath. Mindful of the noxious odors emanating from his trade, Heath situated his modest shop on the outskirts of the village. Days passed with the pungent scent of curing hides permeating the air, accompanied by the rhythmic clattering of hammers against leather as Heath diligently worked to remove any remnants of flesh or fat. Preferring not to offend the villagers' senses, he allowed days, sometimes weeks, to elapse before bringing his completed projects to the village trading posts.

His attire bore the stains of animal urine and dung, the soil and gore of raw hides, and the lingering stench of death. Yet, from this unsavory process emerged exquisite creations—a testament to the dignified resurrection of once-lifeless skins. Bags, harnesses, tacks, armor, quivers, boots, and sandals were among Heath's repertoire, ironically including skins used to carry water for travelers who steered clear of his malodorous tannery.

Despite Heath's renown for crafting the finest leather goods in the region, his trade faced relentless competition. Unscrupulous traders introduced lower-quality hides to the local markets, challenging Heath's commitment to quality and fairness. Villagers accustomed to paying premium prices found themselves tempted by cheaper alternatives, only to discover that such inferior hides lacked durability. Squirrels, beaver pelts, and even dogs were sacrificed on the table of trade to save a shilling. As the saying goes, "They who pay the least often pay the most," for the cost of replacing subpar goods surpasses the initial savings.

One evening, with the setting sun casting long shadows over Thornbridge's cobblestone streets, Heath contemplated his plight. Seeking not only prosperity, but also integrity in his trade, he heard rumors of a wise sage named Elwic residing in the burgeoning town of Havenbrook. Elwic's name had been whispered in songs, portraying him as a recluse with profound insights to share. Heath wondered if this sage could indeed offer the guidance he sought—"The Sage of Havenbrook, the only one, it would be none other than the carpenters' son" as the minstrels sang.

Heath's determination to unlock the mysteries of his trade fueled his nocturnal journey. Through dense forests and across babbling brooks, he ventured until he arrived at the bustling streets of Havenbrook. He inquired upon arrival where he might find the sage, the teacher of wisdom of eternal age. The dwellers were happy to oblige and pointed the traveler to where he did lodge – The tower at the end of the longest path – the path to wisdom and truth.

As he traversed the thoroughfares, Heath was heartened to spot merchants carrying the very leather satchels he had crafted. Recognizing his own patterns and stitches, he felt a sense of pride, knowing that his creations had found their way beyond Thornbridge. Approaching the tower, he observed the flags adorning the cobblestone streets, each bearing symbols universally understood. Two overlapping rings symbolized Chastity, while a scale represented Justice. Charity was depicted by two hands, while Humility and Kindness, though similar, bore distinct differences. These symbols resonated with Heath, imbuing him with a sense of belonging and fostering a spirit of creative cooperation that assuaged the competitive turmoil within him.

Amidst the bustling town, filled with smiles, laughter, and the fragrant aroma of frankincense and lavender, Havenbrook appeared as a paradise to Heath. He eventually reached the ring of rocks before the tower, where the scent of burnt charcoal and ashes enveloped him like a familiar embrace. Reminiscent of his youth, when his father would light a fire each evening to cleanse the day's scent of death from his tanning work, the aroma stirred nostalgic memories within him.

Lost in reverie, Heath was startled by the voice of Elwic emanating from the tower entrance, drawing him back to the present moment.

"Traveler! You seek me. Is there trouble in your heart?" greeted Elwic as Heath approached.

Heath was taken aback by the directness of the sage's question. "You are Elwic, the Sage of Havenbrook?" he inquired.

"I am indeed," affirmed Elwic, a venerable figure with a long, white and black peppered beard and piercing dark eyes.

"Come, come into the tower," Elwic beckoned, waving Heath forward. "I have the finest tea to share with you. It is dried by the tea maker Anika. As skilled as you are in the art of tannery, she is a master of her craft."

Heath paused, momentarily surprised. "How do you know I am a tanner?"

Elwic chuckled, "You smell like one!"

Heath hesitated, but only briefly, before smiling and laughing. "Yes, I suppose I do."

The two men entered the darkened entrance of the tower, greeted by tapestries adorning every wall. These intricate works of art, spanning from floor to ceiling, showcased a diverse array of colors, symbols, and patterns from cultures across the globe.

"Do you like them?" Elwic inquired, gesturing toward the tapestries. "They are all gifts and serve multiple purposes. Can you think of one purpose they serve?"

Heath stuttered, "Um, I suppose it helps keep the drafts out and the warm air in."

Elwic smiled warmly. "Indeed, an excellent observation. If you examine any creation closely, you'll notice more intricate details than initially apparent. Please, walk toward one and tell me what you see."

Heath was drawn to a somber scene depicted in moss greens and blood-red threads. A father led a group of hunters into a dense forest, their dogs straining at their leashes. Meanwhile, a smaller man gazed in another direction, sensing a potential threat. A woman trailed behind, tears streaming down her face as she carried a swaddled baby on her back. The father, his face etched with worry, held a spear, his gaze fixed on a child's half-eaten body in a tree while a lioness lurked nearby. The tragic tale unfolded before Heath's eyes—the child had been carried away into the forest, prompting the father to rally villagers to search for the missing youngster.

"Does it move you?" Elwic interjected, breaking the silence as Heath absorbed the scene.

"Yes, it does. Was it a gift to you?" Heath inquired.

Elwic nodded solemnly. "Indeed. The man with the spear hailed from the Kingdom of Ceraso. His wife, depicted carrying the baby, was gravely ill. He sought my counsel briefly before a hasty departure. Seven seasons later, this tapestry arrived, accompanied by a scroll detailing the family's fate. Christen of Ceraso lost his child and wife but finds solace in their memory. He sends his gratitude and this gift."

"What guidance did you offer?" Heath asked, intrigued.

"Life is transient," Elwic began, his voice tinged with wisdom. "It is a gift entrusted to us for a fleeting moment. Our loved ones, like flickering candle flames, are here for a time, then return to the maker. Cherish the moments, for they are but whispers in the wind." He sighed. His words were laden with the weight of experience.

Heath shifted his gaze away from Elwic and directed it towards another tapestry. This one was crafted with brighter dyed threads – yellows, reds, and soft hues of blue. A woman sat gracefully on an upright log, her blue attire flowing seamlessly from her breasts, accentuating her waist, and draping elegantly to the ground. Her golden hair was intricately braided, adorned with a red burlet atop her head – a symbol of modest wealth and cleanliness. A majestic falcon perched on her left arm, a vigilant guardian, while a slumbering puppy lay curled at her feet. Standing before her was a man garbed in regal attire, his frilly white tunic adorned with a crimson cape. His belt, emblazoned with the colors of the king's family crest, hinted at his royal lineage. Despite his cautious step forward, he held a curious object in his right hand – a heart plucked from his own chest, offered as a token to the maiden, hers to accept or refuse.

"Does this tapestry resonate with you?" Elwic whispered.

Heath nodded. "Indeed. The man presents his beating heart to the woman he loves, yet he remains alive."

"Ah, astute observation! That shall lead us to the reason for your journey to Havenbrook. Please, be seated." Elwic gestured towards an upright log. "Now, tell me, what turmoil troubles your heart?"

"I have built a thriving business, renowned for crafting the finest leather in the entire Kingdom. Merchants from distant lands seek out my wares, and I even spied a satchel of my making upon a traveler's shoulder here in Havenbrook!" Heath exclaimed, his eyes widening with pride.

Elwic stroked his beard thoughtfully. "It is evident that you take great pride in your work."

"Yes, indeed! I am unparalleled in my craft," Heath replied eagerly. "However, my joy has been overshadowed by the emergence of rival tanners who prioritize speed over quality. They neglect the meticulous processes that ensure longevity, failing to soak the rawhides for the necessary duration or properly remove the fat. Their disregard for the traditions of our trade is evident, as they offer inferior goods at lower prices. Their sole concern seems to be the clink of silver, with little regard for the artistry and integrity of our craft."

"And why does this concern you?" Elwic inquired.

"It concerns me because they lack..." Heath paused, collecting his thoughts. "They lack the passion for their craft."

Elwic nodded. "In the first tapestry depicting the child devoured in the forest, the father endured the loss of his entire family—his firstborn child, his wife, and his second child. He grieved deeply, but with time, he found acceptance and gratitude for the moments he shared with his loved ones. Your business is akin to your family, and you feel as though you are losing a part of yourself. Your heart aches, and you mourn. Allow yourself to grieve fully. Let your tears cleanse your spirit. Let your tears soak your flesh and when you have emptied yourself of emotion, let reason prevail. Life persists despite the pain. While you may not be able to alter your competitors' practices, you can reshape the perception of your offerings in the market. Demonstrate to traders, villagers, and traveling merchants how your leather endures through the seasons. Though they may pay a premium for your brand, they will find themselves purchasing multiple items from your competitors over time, as the inferior quality of their goods becomes apparent. Your tapestry will depict generations proudly carrying your leather satchels, a testament to their durability and worth. You see, Heath, your competitor is akin to a hunter seeking whom they may devour."

Elwic rose to stretch his back, his appreciation evident. "I adore this tower," he breathed deeply, his gaze sweeping the circular room. "During my time as a guest of Magister at the Temple of Wisdom and Truth, virtue flags adorned every wall, archway, and doorway. Here in Havenbrook, we share those virtues, rotating them to remind ourselves of their influence on our actions. Yet, in this tower—ah, the tapestries from across the world weave the essence of virtue into their very fabric. Look once more at the second tapestry that caught your eye. It is no coincidence that your soulful gaze was drawn to these two particular pieces."

Heath's gaze lingered on the regally attired man, cautiously offering his heart to the maiden—beside her, a falcon perched on her wrist, and a sleeping puppy at her feet.

Elwic resumed his seat and continued speaking. "The second tapestry also mirrors your journey, Heath. The maiden symbolizes every customer you've ever served. The falcon embodies the skepticism inherent in us all, wary of being deceived and in need of a guardian's protection. The slumbering puppy signifies trust in her decisions. The royal man presents the most precious gift he possesses—his very heart. Heath, your heart beats and bleeds for the essence of who you are and what you stand for. You are Heath the Tanner, the fisherman who draws customers to himself. Your loyal patrons are the cornerstone of your enduring success."

Heath felt a burden lift from his heart.

"Craftsmanship transcends mere skillful hands, Heath," the sage reflected. "It's the fusion of your heart with your craft that defines true mastery. To excel in your trade, you must comprehend not only the properties of leather but also the souls of those who wear it. Above all, recognize the value you bring to the marketplace. Though others may enjoy temporary triumphs or remain persistent nuisances, you will be celebrated as the paragon of quality and integrity in business. While they hunt for prey, Heath, you, my friend, are the fisherman, attracting the righteous to your side."

Elwic continued to impart fundamental insights to Heath, guiding him to see beyond the superficial aspects of his craft. He spoke of empathy and understanding, urging the tanner to discern the unique narratives woven into each piece of leather. Heath absorbed the sage's teachings eagerly, akin to a parched land quenching its thirst with rain.

Armed with newfound wisdom, Heath returned to the village of Thornbridge, his mind teeming with inspiration. He applied Elwic's guidance, infusing his creations with deeper meaning. The villagers were astounded by the transformation, and Heath's renown surged. His leather goods transcended mere accessories; they became conduits for stories and emotions.

News of Heath's rejuvenation as a tanner spread far and wide, captivating merchants and nobles from distant realms. Thornbridge's once modest tannery blossomed into a bastion of artisanal excellence, drawing patrons from across the realm. Heath, the Tanner, was able to reap a harvest from the seeds of excellence he had sown in the morrows of many past sorrows.

As the years passed, Heath's prosperity endured and flourished. The sage's teachings, ingrained into the very fabric of the village's artisan culture, propelled Thornbridge to unprecedented heights.

Thus, in the heart of a medieval village, a tanner named Heath learned that true mastery surpassed mere skill—it necessitated a deep connection between craft and soul, wisdom bestowed upon him by the sage of Havenbrook.

CHAPTER 12

SHADOWS OF ALLEGIANCE

"Greetings, my son. Your troubled countenance betrays the weight of a heavy burden. What troubles you?"

His name was Daniel.

"Dear Elwic, I bear the weight of a false accusation, woven into a sticky spider's web of rumors spun by others from the branch of one twig to the tree of my village. I yearn to defend my honor yet find my resolve waning. I dread the tarnishing of my name in the absence of a fair trial. Will there be a voice to champion my cause in my stead?"

The Sage of Havenbrook regarded the distressed youth with a nod, his breath a quiet exhale in the dimly lit tower room. "Ah, the treacherous path of deceitful tongues is fraught with peril," he mused, his fingers grazing his beard in contemplation. Known for his calculated demeanor, he subtly beckoned the student closer, inviting him to delve deeper into the intricacies of the situation.

"My son, sit with me. Together, let us unravel the tangled web of falsehoods that ensnare you." His motions portrayed the clearing of a spider's work above his head. "Speak the truth as you perceive it."

"In the distant village of Risingdom, a day's journey hence

traveling south," he pointed to the direction. "There are whispers that accuse me of transgressing the sacred tenets of the chapel. Yet, I swear upon all that is sacred, I am innocent of such accusations! The stain upon my name is a grievous injustice," the youth explained.

Elwic's response was measured yet resolute. "False accusations are the venom that poisons the well of justice, young one. But despair not, for today we shall fashion a shield of wisdom to deflect these arrows. Will you heed my counsel, open your mind to knowledge, though painful, and allow my words to light the path ahead?"

Daniel experienced a clash of emotions as peace and torment converged within him. However, the sight of Elwic's solemn and serene eyes acted as a balm to his turmoil. He was prepared to accept the taste of wisdom, though bitter on the tongue of reason. "I am willing," he replied, adopting the demeanor of a grateful pupil.

Elwic's smile was reassuring. "Excellent! To begin, you must grasp the essence of shadows. In the darkness, our adversaries' falsehoods and rumors thrive like bodiless specters. Realizing that you are not beholden to the caprices of the void is the first step toward empowerment. You are liberated from anything not of your own creation."

"But esteemed mentor, how can I dispel these shadowy apparitions, these formless phantoms? I find myself ensnared by the threads of spoken words and their twisted implications."

"Patience, my son," Elwic counseled. "Patience is the lantern that illuminates the truth. Often, when the tale of misfortune is first recounted, reason is cast aside as an inconvenience, a bothersome obstacle that might mar the simplicity of a convenient narrative." He snickered, "Truth could disrupt the mirth of a pithy message, though it be harmful to the soul. Though the narrow passage of the ear, few arrest the first words as the danger it is, rather the words are entreated with delight. Emotion seizes control, mercilessly subjugating truth to an emotional response of any audience. Patience is the virtue that rescues the heart from hasty judgment. Few possess the wisdom to recognize the heart as a vessel more fragile than the mind, which alone is capable of dispensing justice. When faced with accusations, maintain your composure. Speak with clarity and conviction, but do not let anger dictate your actions. Your intellect will be the force that proclaims and reveals the truth to all, even if not in your immediate presence. Your reputation will transcend the cacophony of gossip."

Daniel absorbed Elwic's words with earnestness, though a shadow of doubt lingered, prompting a question. "The villagers of Risingdom have already condemned me. How can mere words sway their entrenched beliefs?"

Words alone may prove insufficient," Elwic asserted, straightening his posture like a poised mantis ready to strike with wisdom. "Actions, my son, serve as the anvil upon which perceptions are shaped. Persist in your quest for truth, and let your deeds bear witness to your innocence. Have faith that fate will eventually deliver you from this trial."

Daniel bowed his head, longing to break free from the prison of public opinion. "And what of those who conspired in this deception? Should they not face judgment?" he demanded.

Elwic sighed wearily. "The allure of vengeance is strong, but tread cautiously. Pursue not retribution, but rather seek redemption. Beware the snare of bitterness—the darkest seed that grows unchecked. It yields poisonous fruit, corrupting the soul once filled with light and joy. Instead, illuminate the path of truth, and let justice be the judge of their actions. It is not your burden, nor your responsibility, to mete out another's conscience. Just as the waves of the ocean obey natural law, so also are the actions of humanity to sow their own consequences. A breeze may become the tempest, an acorn may become a forest, and a seed of anger may blossom into death—a debt that consumes flesh and bone until naught remains."

Pausing for emphasis, Elwic continued, "Daniel, live with integrity. Provide no cause for your innocence to be challenged."

"O Wise Sage of Havenbrook," Daniel choked back tears,

"your words weigh heavy upon me, and I feel my strength falter. Can you offer words to mend my wounded heart and restore hope? When I return to the village gates, will those who know me stand as witnesses for my cause?"

Elwic's response was solemn and measured. "I must speak the truth as I know it, even if it is not always easy to hear. It's true that others may not rush to your defense. Despite their claims of loyalty, when faced with the test, true friends might not prioritize your well-being or the defense of your reputation. Perhaps safeguarding your character is not their foremost concern. Even if you are innocent, associating with the accused may bring them discomfort as they fear being unfairly judged alongside you. These friends are for sharing the alehouse table, your stories of travel, or the celebration of your baby's birth, but the troubled times," Elwic shook his head, "The troubled times are costly. It may mean sacrifice of food, income, sharing their roof, or worse, speaking out to preserve your honor." The sage stood and stretched his arms above his head. He breathed in deep and let out a sigh. He sat down and spoke with a stern tone.

"It is nearly impossible to rely on verbal testimony to safeguard your honor. Your friends, alas, often yield to convenience. Loyalty, it seems, holds little weight. Do you hold such expectations? Then, I fear they are founded on false hope. Despite the potential for their words to exonerate you and affirm your rightful place, they cower like trembling kittens in the presence of narcissistic rulers. If you must feel anything, let it not be the sting of betrayal but rather the pity for their weakness. Their boastful mouths merely reveal the feebleness of spirit in times of adversity. You, on the other hand, possess true strength!

Those who speak loudly yet shrink from action are not to be trusted; they are mere pawns, ensnared by their own hopeless and helpless consciences. Accept in your heart that feeble men are foolish chatterers, seeking favor from their oppressors and not with the virtues that would save them when they fall into a desperate pit."

"But could there not still be some cause for anguish?" Daniel pleaded for solace.

"Yes and no," Elwic responded. "You can liberate yourself from the shackles of another's frivolous narrative. The stage they set, the script they write, and the actors they employ are none of your concern. Unless you willingly participate in their drama, you can be a free spirit, unbound by their chains. I offer you a path to liberation, a journey of forgiveness, and the strength of resilience. Cast off the burden of guilt unjustly placed upon you —it is not a cloak you are meant to wear. Live out the principles of virtue, the path of wisdom, and the creed of integrity, and the false accusations will dissolve like water off a duck's back. If you are truly pure, innocent of the allegations against you, the truth will eventually come to light, and your name will be vindicated."

Daniel collapsed before Elwic, the Sage of Havenbrook, curling into a ball upon the hard earth. His knees pressed into the ground, fists pounding the soil on either side of his head as tears streamed down his cheeks, mingling with the earth below.

"It is time, Daniel, to rest. Under the sheltering wings of wisdom, your inner resolve will triumph over external adversaries. This may not be your final encounter with the shadows of deceit. Those who aspire to walk the path of virtue often become targets for those who fall short of righteousness. Though you may sometimes falter, the purity within your heart mourns when darkness oppresses the innocent. When the light reveals darkness, your heart rejoices. Seek that justice and though it may seem unpopular, time will reveal the truth. Remember, grace is renewed with each dawn—may you extend that gift even to your enemies."

And so it was. Daniel awoke the following day refreshed in body and renewed in spirit. He faced the day head-on with vigor unseen since his retreat to Havenbrook. Returning to the village of his accusers, he found only one voice speaking ill of him, but it was met with indifference. His character spoke louder than the slander of his detractors. Resolved and confident, he reclaimed his rightful place in the community. His name was vindicated, and those who had tormented him became objects of suspicion whenever they spoke. Their lies, once public, now withered into mere whispers drowned out by the serum of truth. They dared not besmirch him again. "Those who know, know!" became a rallying cry among the wise, confidently silencing the slithering tongues of slanderers.

And so it was that the Sage of Havenbrook imparted the timeless principles he had gleaned from the Temple of Wisdom and Truth. Daniel absorbed these teachings and, in turn, reflected the peace of prose that had nourished his soul. His life became a testament to the power of words. His testimony illuminated the dark recesses of people's hearts where the Sage himself could not tread. And so, it shall be with you.

Take lessons from these tales, embrace the truth, and share the wisdom with others, say I, Actar, the scribe of Havenbrook.

CHAPTER 13

ALARIC THE FARMER

THE DIM LIGHT OF DAWN BROKE, ACCOMPANIED BY THE DISTANT crow of a rooster. His call echoed the established hierarchy, a signal to his flock and a warning of potential threats that the guardian of the domain was vigilant and prepared to defend. Just as craftsmen proudly displayed their wares each morning, boasting of quality and skill, so too did this confident rooster proclaim, "Come to my domain, where the finest treasures await your trade.

Many relied on nature's bounty to sustain their livelihoods: the weaver with sheep's wool, the candle maker with beeswax plundered from honeycombs, the miller grinding wheat with a stone. There were blacksmiths shaping metals, physicians blending herbs, and butchers providing sustenance from the land's creatures.

Among them was Alaric, a farmer whose patience was as steadfast as his fields. His work spanned from early spring to late autumn, each season crucial to his livelihood. But this particular year, fortune turned against him. Despite his diligence, the harvest was meager, and scarcity threatened to steal the fruits of his labor. Concerned for his family and village, Alaric pondered the fate of his business.

While the butchers preserved dried meat for lean times, Alaric's crops of radishes, wheat, spelled, onions, and beans were essential for nourishing the community's appetite. Though communal efforts sustained many, Alaric was a pillar of Grimsby, tirelessly tending his fields day and night, hoping for a miracle to rescue his wilting crops. But as a relentless drought parched the earth, his once-fertile fields lay barren and dry. Yet, Alaric, with a spirit as resilient as his land, refused to surrender to despair.

He yearned for guidance. Thoughts of the revered Sage of Havenbrook, Elwic, filled his mind, and as the next morning dawned, Alaric embarked on his journey to seek counsel with destiny. Four days passed until the Tower of Havenbrook appeared in the distance. Fueled by hope for wisdom or, at the very least, a comforting word, Alaric quickened his pace as dusk descended over the mountains, casting a dwindling natural light upon his path. Would he arrive in time to meet the Sage? Would the Sage be willing to offer guidance when Alaric knocked on his door? Or would there be time for him?

These questions tormented him, yet he resolved to press on, determined to uncover the answers he sought.

As he approached the outskirts of Havenbrook, shanties and shacks came into view, lining a muddy path with their haphazard construction. Despite their dilapidation, signs of poverty were overshadowed by an underlying sense of hope and anticipation. Each humble dwelling seemed to represent a starting point, a stepping stone toward a brighter future. Continuing onward, Alaric observed a gradual transition in the architecture and atmosphere of the town. Cobblestone streets replaced mud, while sturdy rock foundations lent a sense of permanence to the buildings that stood taller and prouder, declaring their endurance.

Suddenly, a bright red banner adorned with a white sword caught Alaric's attention. Positioned diagonally, the sword pointed skyward, away from the shutter to which it was affixed. Spotting the first inhabitant of the town, Alaric inquired, pointing to the banner, "What does this symbol mean?"

The individual glanced up momentarily before returning their gaze to Alaric. "It represents the virtue of courage," they replied. Without hesitation, they suddenly exclaimed, "CHARGE!" Raising an arm dramatically as if facing an invisible foe, they then dropped the imaginary sword by their side and burst into laughter, accompanied by a wheezing from their chest.

Alaric cleared his throat. "Could you perhaps direct me to the Sage of Havenbrook?" he asked politely.

The clown responded promptly, "Of course! Follow the light!" A bony finger extended, pointing towards a distant fire. Alaric nodded his thanks before hurrying off in the indicated direction. As he left, he heard the clown cry out, "Charge!" once more, pointing their imaginary sword at the night sky before disappearing into the darkness, their laughter fading away into a scattered wheezing cough.

Alaric's heart quickened with anticipation. Soon, he would seek guidance from one who could help alleviate the hardships his village of Grimsby faced, while Havenbrook thrived. With each step closer to the town center, the surroundings became more vibrant and colorful. Tall buildings, two or three stories high, lined the cobblestone streets, adorned with numerous banners. It felt as though a perpetual carnival had taken up residence in Havenbrook, with colors dancing from door to door.

The town bustled with life, murmuring voices mixing with hearty laughter and the clinking of brass cups from nearby alehouses. Bells around the necks of passing animals added to the lively atmosphere, while the sizzle of frying potato cakes outside a rustic eatery provided a low, savory undertone to the symphony of humanity. Havenbrook pulsed with vitality. He breathed in deeply and paused his march at the smell of the potato cakes. They teased his stomach, but his hunger and thirst for knowledge quenched the desire so as not to be distracted by a temporal pleasure – "better to eat and drink wisdom than dine on the victuals of fools." His father once said to him; that day so long ago when he was given the chance to read an ancient script instead of gathering rumors into his ears from the village wagglemouth.

Alaric located the crackling bonfire just outside the Tower door and hesitantly decided to knock. After a moment's hesitation, he knocked again, leaning in close to peer through a crack in the door. Inside, a flickering shadow moved about, while the invitational scent of frankincense reached his nose. Startled by a sigh, Alaric jerked his head back, fearing the door might open while he leaned against it, but nothing happened. Slowly, he resumed his cautious approach, pressing his lips as close to the crack as possible and spoke softly, "Lord Elwic, I beg an audience with you."

Alaric withdrew from the crack and peered inside, only to find darkness where there had once been light and shadows. Confused, he noticed what he thought was a shaggy coat of fur. Suddenly, a voice broke the silence, asking, "Who seeks an audience?"

Startled, Alaric stumbled backward, landing on the ground. Elwic had somehow moved to the other side of the door, revealing that the coat of fur was his frothy beard. As the door swung open with a rush of wind, Alaric gasped, his mouth agape at the imposing figure of the Sage towering over him, his piercing eyes framed by bushy eyebrows and lines of wisdom etched into his face. Yet, there was a glorious aura about him. "I asked you a question. Who seeks an audience?" Elwic inquired again.

Collecting himself, Alaric quickly exhaled before responding, "It is I, Alaric the farmer."

Elwic nodded, recognizing the humble tone of a man connected to the earth, a hero of every village. "Ah! Another visitor from outside of Havenbrook," he observed.

"No, I am not just from outside Havenbrook. I come from

Grimsby. I have traveled four days, seeking your wisdom with every step," Alaric explained earnestly.

The Sage admired the farmer's determination. "As the ancient text says, 'Seek and you shall find,'" Elwic mused. "You knocked, and my door opened. Now, I suppose you have a question?" he added with a chuckle.

"I do," Alaric blurted out. "I am desperate and on the verge of despair. I seek your counsel."

Elwic extended his hand, offering Alaric assistance from the earth to stand alongside him. Alaric accepted the gesture, surprised by the strength and firm grip of Elwic's hand. He hadn't realized the Sage was also a carpenter, a man intimately connected with wood and creation.

"Sit by the fire," Elwic suggested, pointing to a bench. "Soon, the townsfolk will gather, but for now, let us spend some quiet time together." As Alaric settled onto the bench, Elwic continued, "I built this with my own hands, and the splinters remain as reminders. Just as you have dirt under your fingernails, I have not forgotten my origins or where I shall return. And you, Alaric, will return to Grimsby with purpose and design. So, what does a farmer seek from a Sage? My seeds are for the mind; yours are for the soil."

Alaric marveled at the wisdom in Elwic's words. "Perhaps you may have heard of the tragedy that has befallen us. Our crops have failed, our fields are dry. While we have enough to sustain us through the winter and into the next harvest, if the land remains barren, I fear the worst. I know the dirt and dust of my days, but you, Sage of Havenbrook, understand the minds and souls of men. Whether it's treasure or guidance I seek, my question remains: What should I do?"

Elwic contemplated for a moment before posing a question of his own. "When you dig and plant a seed, what is your first thought?"

Alaric pondered briefly. "My first thought is always, 'What is best for the seed, the soil, and the rain?' I consider the earth, the potential garden of what's to come."

"Ah, so you see before it is seen," Elwic remarked, delving deeper into the farmer's perspective.

Elwic's crinkles and wrinkles twinkled with amusement as he addressed the excited farmer. "Stay here for tonight's teachings. You'll find a bed in the Tower and provisions for your return journey."

Delving into a small pouch at his waist, Elwic retrieved a coin and handed it to Alaric. Engraved upon it were three consecutive numbers: 777.

Alaric received the gift with apprehension. "Kind Lord! I came not to receive a gift, but rather to beg for your wisdom!"

Elwic nodded, "I know your heart and I have begun our lesson with the ancient text – the ancient text found in the book of seven letters, the seventh chapter and the seventh verse: 777. You will understand soon."

Minutes after their private conversation concluded, the teachings commenced. The bustling sounds of the town faded into silence; no more clinking of brass cups, no more chiming of animal bells. Elwic's soothing voice resonated, imparting lessons on asking, seeking, and knocking. He shared stories of a farmer in need of wisdom, emphasizing the importance of seeking not just for oneself but for the greater good of the community. Virtues such as caring, determination, and integrity were elucidated with clarity, accompanied by practical applications that resonated with all. Alaric found himself immersed in the beauty of the moment as the townsfolk waved flags symbolizing the virtues, transforming the teachings into a sensory experience. He heard the instructions and visualized them vividly. His quest was to ask, seek, and knock on every door without the righteous ego to thwart the progress or answer he needed.

That night, Alaric struggled to sleep, his mind abuzz with anticipation for the future. He envisioned unlocking the deep reservoirs with the assistance of the community. As dawn broke, he rose eagerly, but Elwic was nowhere to be found. The explanation offered for his absence was that he had ventured into the woods at dawn to spend time with the Spirit.

On the eighth day of his journey, Alaric returned to his home village, bursting with news of his findings. He swiftly summoned a messenger, and under the shade of a majestic oak tree, an assembly was called.

"Oh, good people of Grimsby," Alaric began, his voice imbued with newfound purpose. "I have discovered a path to ensure our survival amidst these harsh times. We need not resign ourselves to the mercy of nature. Instead, we shall adapt!"

Curiosity mingled with skepticism in the air, yet Alaric's fervor proved infectious. He asked questions of all the villagers, and their minds began to open with ideas. No longer were they subject to what was but became obsessed with what could be. One idea sparked another, and another idea was born, and then another. Their minds were exponentially expanded.

With a sparkle in his eye and the faith of many, an innovation was outlined to construct an intricate network of underground tunnels, designed to channel water from hidden springs to irrigate the fields.

This innovative approach would enable the village to cultivate crops even in the face of droughts or other adversities. Provisions were made to capture rainwater and store it in strategic locations, ensuring every resident had access—to a veritable library of water.

Initially met with skepticism from the village leaders who lived under the cloak of doubt and fear, Alaric's proposal gained momentum as he tirelessly labored alongside his fellow villagers to realize his vision. With pickaxes and shovels, they delved deep into the earth, crafting a labyrinth of tunnels beneath the fields. Though arduous, their determination was fueled by the hope of a bountiful harvest. As they dug, sweat buckets, and sang praises, their dedicated labor was rewarded by the cheers and admiration of those who could not lift a shovel or axe. The high morale was an integral pillar of strength and a balm of healing when the muscles pleaded for rest and retirement from the hard work of carving into the earth.

As seasons passed, Alaric's underground irrigation system proved its worth. Crops flourished, transforming once-barren fields into expanses of golden wheat and lush vegetables. Grimsby, once on the brink of starvation, now teemed with life and prosperity.

Alaric's ingenuity not only saved Grimsby from famine but also catalyzed its transformation into a thriving community. His steadfast resolve and resourcefulness sowed the seeds of a future marked by abundance and well-being.

News of Alaric's triumph spread far and wide, earning admiration from neighboring villages and even the king's court. He emerged as a folk hero, a testament to the resilience of the human spirit. His unwavering faith in the face of adversity stood as a beacon of hope, demonstrating that human ingenuity could triumph over the most formidable challenges posed by nature.

One day, as Alaric gazed over the expansive fields of Grimsby, a young boy approached him. "Lord Alaric, what wisdom can you impart to me, a humble boy?"

Alaric reached into a small pouch at his waist and retrieved a coin inscribed with three consecutive numbers: 777.

"There are treasures and reservoirs beyond what meets the eye," he began. "The greatest counsel I can offer is this: When we delve deep into the soil of our minds and hearts, when we ask, answers shall come. When we seek, we shall find. And when you knock, doors shall open."

As the years passed, the memory of Alaric, the medieval farmer who defied the odds, endured in the hearts of Grimsby's grateful inhabitants. His coin became a cherished heirloom, passed down through generations, a symbol of wisdom and resilience, and a symbol of the ancient text found in the "Book of Seven Letters", the seventh chapter and the seventh verse.

CHAPTER 14

OF HUMILITY AND FORGIVENESS

"GONG, GONG, GONG", RESONATED THE TOWER'S BRASS BELL. A wisp of cold air trailed, weaving through narrow channels of cobblestone streets and muddy alleys. Ears perked, attuned to the call. Without protest, many a sedentary figure leaped into motion, drawn to the source. Amidst a camaraderie of subdued laughter and eager anticipation, foundational emotions permeated the gathering, settling into a tranquil and reverent assembly before the master.

In the dimly lit halls of knowledge, where wisdom flowed like a gentle stream, the medieval sage expounded his teachings on humility, extolling it as the cornerstone of genuine wisdom and enlightenment. With a gentle and wise voice, he addressed his disciples:

"Seekers of truth, come close and heed my words, for today we shall plumb the depths of humility. Understand that humility is not a badge of weakness or lack of confidence; rather, it is a virtue that nurtures the very core of our being. It is the fertile soil from which true wisdom sprouts and flourishes."

"Envision, my dear students, a towering oak tree that stretches towards the heavens. Its branches sway gracefully, its leaves dancing with the wind. Yet, as grand as the oak may be, it bows humbly to the earth, its roots firmly entrenched in the soil. So too is humility - it allows us to stand tall while remaining anchored in our origins."

The Sage paused, allowing his words to resonate within the hearts and minds of his disciples. Then he continued:

"In a world where pride and arrogance often cloud reason, humility serves as a guiding beacon, illuminating the path to genuine knowledge. It teaches us to recognize that our achievements and understanding are mere droplets in the vast ocean of wisdom that lies ahead.

Let us not emulate the fool who, intoxicated by his own perceived greatness, fails to grasp the true enormity of the universe. Instead, let us emulate the humble scholar who, with each step along the path of learning, realizes the vastness of what remains unknown."

The sage's voice resonated with reverence and humility as he continued:

"To embrace humility is to acknowledge that every individual we encounter possesses a unique perspective and knowledge that surpasses our own. Within their stories and experiences lie lessons that can enrich our understanding. Let us, therefore, approach others with respect, for even the most unassuming among them may hold a treasure of wisdom yet unearthed.

As we navigate life's journey, let humility accompany us as a steadfast companion. It tempers our ego and fosters empathy within us. Through humility, we come to recognize the interconnectedness of all existence and to treasure the beauty inherent in every humble corner of creation.

Consider the ant, in its diminutive size, it exemplifies remarkable wisdom. While summer reigns, it diligently prepares for winter. Study the ant and its ways, and gain wisdom. Governed not by external authority but by instinct, it naturally does what is right without consideration of self. Yet, inevitably, there comes the end of the season, and with it, the sluggard, whose negligence leaves them hungry and astonished at their plight. If only they would heed the simplicity of labor and the foresight of preparation for winter. If only they would embrace the reward of serving the land, humbling themselves to touch it, to feel it crumble in their hands, and to inhale the fragrance of that which will outlive their mortal frame. Advocating for all is not only an act of altruism but also self-preservation. Humility is not weakness, but strength."

As usual, there was always one among the gathering who questioned the wisdom of Elwic's teachings. This individual raised his hand, the question masked in innocence but laden with arrogance.

"I am a member of a society. We lead our village and many others, overseeing them for the common good. We rule by virtue of our ancestral heritage and superior wisdom. Must humility be a virtue we adhere to? To be frank, all this talk seems unnecessary when dealing with the lower class."

Elwic remained steadfast, his expression unwavering. The question posed lacked empathy, compassion, and benevolence. It bore the mark of selfishness, a trait deeply ingrained in the man. To prioritize others' needs over his own was an enigma to him. Hunger was an unfamiliar concept; fasting or enduring deprivation held no significance. This "ruler" was feeble, his aging body falsely elevated above his soul, spirit, and clarity of mind. He couldn't grasp the value of humility, as foreign to him as an obscure language. His world was confined by narrow perspectives perpetuated by limited minds. Blinded by ego, he failed to perceive common sense, a sense that could shield him from peril and future harm.

"No," Elwic declared. Any investment in knowledge or generosity seemed futile, akin to casting resources into an abyss of darkness; casting pearls before swine. The traveler's ignorance was profound, his request a veiled attempt to shirk responsibility. Elwic's response left no room for excuse or argument; every virtue of humility stood as an unyielding guardian. His words began to flow:

"Humility nurtures a profound respect for others,

irrespective of their social standing. It prompts individuals to extend kindness and empathy to all, fostering communal harmony."

Elwic drew a cleansing breath before continuing, "Forgiveness," he uttered, emphasizing the word. "A humble soul is inclined to forgive and forget. By acknowledging their own imperfections, one becomes more empathetic toward the faults of others, forging stronger and more compassionate bonds. Failure to do so leads to hypocrisy and restless misery."

Closing his eyes briefly as if to simulate rest, Elwic swiftly reopened them. "To those who have traveled from afar, we shall converse later," he announced, then redirected his attention to the gathering.

"Attend closely," he commanded, rousing the audience. "Servant leadership... Humility in leadership entails prioritizing others' needs above one's own. A humble leader serves their people with sincerity, selflessness, and unwavering loyalty. Respect is not commanded but earned."

Elwic's gaze shifted towards the traveler. "Do you have any inquiries?"

The individual who had raised his hand tightened his lips, shook his head, and lowered his chin in silence.

Elwic continued, his gaze sweeping over the crowd.

"Openness to counsel - now there's a mark of true leadership," he remarked with a shake of his head. "Watch closely, and you'll see that humble leaders welcome advice and seek feedback. Those who don't, pity those under their rule— serving beneath self-absorbed overseers breeds deep wells of resentment and hearts grown cold. Humility in leadership means recognizing one's limitations despite holding a position of authority. It means valuing the ideas, opinions, and perspectives of others, thus earning the trust necessary to lead effectively. Humility fosters a lifelong dedication to learning. Those who approach knowledge humbly remain receptive to new ideas, perspectives, and experiences, even from sources they once dismissed as outdated or uninformed." Elwic paused, a faint chuckle escaping him before he resumed.

"I employ the term 'humility,' yet I wonder if its essence truly resonates as I describe actions reflecting this virtue," he mused, appearing lost in thought. "It's more than mere actions; humility is a state of being, cultivated from a seed planted deep within the heart."

Standing, Elwic stretched his arms above his head, feigning a yawn.

"Are my words wearisome to you?" he inquired of the crowd as sparks danced from the fire into the night sky.

"Press on, Lord Elwic!" came a fervent cry.

Amidst the darkness, pleas for enlightenment echoed. "Teach us! Teach us!"

Seating himself upon the upright log, Elwic drew a deep breath through his nose, exhaling audibly. It was a silent acknowledgment of his weariness, frustration, and exhaustion in imparting lessons of simplicity to a complex audience. Nurturing intellectual and spiritual growth amidst stubborn minds and fickle hearts felt akin to herding cats.

"Rather than boasting, humility prompts individuals to recognize external influences and the contributions of others beyond their personal efforts," he continued, his voice carrying a note of urgency.

"It encourages a humble acceptance of one's limitations, developing a disciplined pursuit of knowledge free from arrogance. Humility enables graceful handling of failure; instead of casting blame, a humble individual takes ownership of mistakes, learns from them, and endeavors to improve. Do you grasp the significance of these lessons? Are you willing to acknowledge the possibility of error in your assumptions? Can you transform the weight of guilt into a catalyst for meaningful change? Are you willing to take the heavy hand of guilt you have brandished and turn it into sorrow that reaps a wealth of change?"

The crowd murmured, but Elwic pressed on.

"Humility compels all citizens to champion social justice. By acknowledging their privileges and empathizing with the less fortunate, humble individuals strive to create a fairer and more equitable society."

The murmurs subsided.

"Consider this: the greatest among you are servants to the least. Those who are least among you hold the greatest significance, serving as poignant reminders of our shared purpose. If you fail to grasp this, your heart is hardened by arrogance and pride. Humility is foreign to you. When the Day of Atonement meets the consequences of greed, you shall reap what you have sown. Your pursuit of justice yields the fruit of pride. True righteousness stems from cause and effect."

Elwic paused, bowing his head slightly.

"A seed yields a harvest of its kind. It is simple logic, yet some remain perplexed. Understand this: the prideful soul meets its demise."

With these words, Elwic concluded his teachings, leaving the gathered crowd with a final admonition:

"Remember, my dear students, that genuine humility seeks not to elevate oneself but to uplift others. It opens the doors to knowledge and understanding, enabling us to become beacons of wisdom and compassion. The world is shrouded in ignorance, and, as long as humanity endures, the need for these truths persists. We must continue to impart these lessons tirelessly."

As the crowd began to disperse, Elwic called out to the one who had first spoken, the leader of the travelers:

"I promised you a conversation," Elwic declared, sitting up with regal poise, setting a somber tone for what was to come. The leader leaned forward, anticipation evident in his expression, unaware of what awaited him.

"I would not subject you to public scrutiny," Elwic continued, "for it might have closed your heart to the truths you need to hear. I see you. I see through you. Not only that, but I see what lies within you."

The leader of the band cocked his head, curling his upper lip in a display of arrogance that belied all of Elwic's previous words. Unfazed, Elwic began to speak.

"You seek forgiveness yet refuse to forgive. You crave to receive yet withhold giving. You demand heat from the fire but offer no wood. Likewise, you yearn for love while nurturing hatred in your heart. You plead for freedom yet hold others captive to their past. Despite their pleas for release, you rattle the chains, a constant reminder of their history, igniting the flames of their anger. Outwardly, you feign innocence, but within, a conniving spirit schemes to tear apart tortured souls.

You long for peace yet sow seeds of discord. You crave respect while tarnishing another's reputation. You whisper shame and gossip about the oppressed who seek redemption. Not only that, but you desire adulation while tarnishing the name of another. You extend no mercy, no grace, no forgiveness, yet wonder why you are shunned by many within your kin. You seek healing yet inflict wounds upon angry dogs without compassion.

This rings true of my kin and of those under our oversight. You speak the truth! I will carry these profound words back to my village. Oh, the tales I could tell of their wicked deeds that leave us speechless around the table. Ha! It's as if you've encountered them face-to-face!"

Elwic's eyes blazed with intensity, akin to a wild boar ensnared by a hunter's trap, snorting and growling with righteous anger. He turned his gaze towards the travelers, especially the leader, unafraid to reveal his fury, sparing no measure of it. With a gaze as piercing as a flame, he spoke with the authority of a lion's roar.

"I have encountered them, and they stand before me," his voice thundered like a lion's roar.

The ground trembled beneath them, loose dirt shimmering uncertainly. Would the earth swallow them whole, or would Elwic, the Sage of Havenbrook, show mercy? Cold chills shivered down the spine of the travelers. As though the God of

Abraham had struck them down and turned them into pillars of salt, they froze in fear and trembled from within. Their skin rippled in waves, a palpable manifestation of the conviction washing over them—a necessary purification of the hidden wickedness they had cloaked as righteousness. The process of refinement was a painful ordeal, but one they must endure. If true wisdom were their quest, they would receive it only after relinquishing much and forsaking their former ways. Otherwise, their spirits risked being crushed and consigned to eternal damnation.

Elwic pressed on, his words cutting through the silence like a sword. "You do not seek wisdom; you seek validation to persist in your sin. Your hearts are veiled from the truth. Wisdom eludes you unless you embrace the necessary agony of repentance."

As the earthquake's tremors subsided into a mournful rumble, stirring the somber air, Elwic's voice lowered to a whisper.

"The ego is a beast that consumes the poison it brews. It brings death without sight of the power it wields. Destruction lies in the tongue, and the heart ruled by ego is shackled to death. You will depart from Havenbrook tonight with hearts hardened or as vessels broken by the conviction of your sin. Your mortal shells will decay more swiftly because of your perverse heart, or if you choose, you may shine with the light of repentance." Elwic spoke but did not wait for a response.

"Here, tonight, you face a choice between death and life. Forgive those who wronged you, even if they do not seek grace or deserve mercy. Renounce your haughty arrogance and the false righteousness of your anger. Cease whispering and reviving dead tales in which there is no life, but offensive odors of rotting flesh. Refrain from besmirching another's reputation until you yourself are faultless. If you have no secret sin of your own, you may throw the stone of accusation at another. And may I say with accuracy, you are not without a sin that hurts a brother, a sister, a member of your cult, and certainly not one who parades among you as a leader!

Your words can either shackle painful memories or bring love, light, and healing to souls longing for freedom. It is your choice. But remember this: your words are seeds sown into an unseen realm, yielding a harvest that you alone will reap. And this question you must ask now that you have been made aware of your actions: will it bring you a life of peace and harmony, or one of pain and destruction? I offer you a choice—alter your path and live or persist in your comfortable ways and perish slowly."

A distant wind howled, approaching the scene with ferocity, but as it reached Elwic's presence, it faltered, dropping to the ground and falling silent. A few leaves rustled by in the aftermath of the halted breeze, but simply unable to become substantial at the feet of the one who spoke the truth.

The leader of the travelers struggled to breathe, his tongue seeming to swell at every attempt to speak. Gasping for air, he found Elwic's words anathema to his mind. Anger surged within him, his heart pounding like a confined thunderstorm. He refused to accept guilt or shame for his actions; it was the fault of others, not his own, he thought to himself. His village, he silently protested, was filled with wretched souls lacking morality and righteousness. Yet, in truth, he was the epitome of self-righteousness and conceit. His piety had blinded him, and now he could no longer plead ignorance. Instead, his ego flared to defend his actions. Blood boiled, the temperature rose, and flashes of anger raced through his body. He had lived his life dictating how others should live, oblivious to his own hypocrisy, a shell of selfish ambition.

The stones around the fire seemed to resonate with the turmoil until a collective wail broke the rocky chorus. Members of the troupe from afar joined in, crying out, "Forgive us! Forgive us!"

However, the leader stood defiant, his heart hardening like stone. Blood flow was impeded by the constricted passages of his veins, pressure mounting within. Clenching his fists and grinding his teeth, he resisted the change overtaking his mortal body. Nearby followers retreated from his trembling form, fearful of an impending explosion. Every muscle contracted, and he shook violently. Then, with a primal scream, he unleashed a roar of defiance, only for it to diminish into a whimper. The proud and arrogant leader, once imposing, now lay as a lifeless heap at Elwic's feet.

The death of ego in the form of flesh. The former followers wrapped the soulless clump and carried him out, shaking their heads at the vanity of his ways. When the fire burned the last remnants of his bones outside the town of Havenbrook, they remembered Elwic's words: "Seekers of truth, come close and heed my words, for today we shall plumb the depths of humility."

Their leader was no leader at all; he was the personification of one who devours the souls of people.

"Let us understand the ways of humility and forgiveness." One cried out.

Another spoke, "We are dust, and this we shall remember as we serve one another."

"And this is a lesson in the crafting of one's soul, as understood by strangers to our land and foes of truth. I write these words so that others may see what the power of thought can become when fully realized."

—Actar, the scribe of Havenbrook.

CHAPTER 15

THE LEATHER BOOK

In times like these, when precious commodities were few and far between, something of immense value was guarded with utmost care. Elwic possessed such a treasure—a weathered leather-bound book filled with the timeless verses of the ages, a collection of Proverbs passed down through generations. These profound sayings, penned by ancient sages, held the secrets to virtuous living and the wisdom to navigate life's myriad challenges. This invaluable tome was known simply as The Book of Wisdom.

Elwic's time in the Temple of Wisdom and Truth remained shrouded in mystery. Many believed that when he ventured up the hill and into the woods, he would return that same night after communing with the nocturnal sounds of owls and wolves. (Not even a knight would sleep alone with all his leather and armor as protection.) However, nights turned into weeks, and weeks into months, with seasons passing without a word from him. Some openly mourned Elwic's supposed demise, spinning tales of his tragic end without a shred of evidence to support their speculations. Some shared versions of his death without evidence, and thus, the fictional tales began. He got lost and starved. A traveler found some bones! Oh no, another gossiper begged attention, He was ravaged as he slept; eaten by the black wolf!

The village blather-mouths contrived stories to fascinate and outdo the next - as was the propensity of human nature, the duty to embellish and create drama for the sake of amusement.

He was said to have perished from starvation or to have fallen prey to a savage beast, each tale more fanciful than the last.

Not just seasons, but years slipped away. Throughout it all, Elwic's father, the village carpenter, held fast to hope for his son's return. Adding to the mystery of Elwic's disappearance was his father's claim that a mysterious visitor, named Magister, had sat in fellowship with him for days while designing the Tower. Though unseen by others in the village, Elwic's father often spoke of this enigmatic figure.

The old man toiled tirelessly, dedicating decades to making endless trips into the woods, meticulously harvesting, cutting, and shaping lumber. Each piece was carefully stacked, with the final ones cut destined to be the first used in constructing the Tower of Havenbrook—an ark of knowledge and a repository of wisdom.

On the eve of his father's passing, Elwic finally returned to Havenbrook. Departing as a boy, he came back a man transformed. While his father had trained him in carpentry, Elwic now wielded a different kind of craftsmanship— knowledge, wisdom, and truth. With him, he brought the greatest of riches—wisdom encapsulated in The Book of Wisdom, a leather-bound tome rarely touched by others and always kept secure in Elwic's hands.

Every week, Elwic gathered the townspeople at the Tower's entrance, sharing the timeless truths from The Book of Wisdom beside the bonfire. Farmers, knights, merchants, and scholars alike eagerly absorbed the pearls of wisdom Elwic had to offer. On one brisk afternoon, as the townspeople gathered, Elwic opened the book and began to speak.

"My friends, let us delve into the ancient words of the wise," he began, the fire crackling fiercely beside him. "Words are the foundation of creation, the essence of our hearts. They hold the power to heal, to guide, and to illuminate. As we explore these verses, we find the light that guides us through life's darkest paths."

With each proverb, Elwic wove tales of everyday life, drawing lessons from the timeless words on the parchment. "Take, for example, this proverb," he paused, "A soft answer turns away wrath, but a harsh word stirs up anger," he explained. "In our interactions, let us choose words that soothe and heal, rather than wound and enrage."

The people listened intently, captivated by Elwic's storytelling and the meaningful wisdom he shared. He continued, "Do you wield words like knives, seeking to harm? Are they weapons of destruction? Resist the urge for revenge when spoken ill of; instead, let your words be waves of healing. Do not battle hate with hate but baptize your enemies in love. Heap kindness upon them, and they will be confounded, and honored by your spirit. Your words hold power - they can bring light or darkness. The tongue has the power of life and death; its use yields fruit—sweetness or bitterness. You desire honey, but you feed your audience the bitterness of a dandelion.

Oh, the marvelous muscle that tastes all manner of beauty and can be the purveyor of truth drips of innocent blood under the villainous sword of lies and gossip. The tongue is a tool of the mind; let your mind serve virtue, truth, honesty, and purity. Bring your mind to servitude. Think about goodness and kindness, for these traits elevate us above barbarity. As I have taught you to be virtuous, and praiseworthy in how you live and how you treat others, these are the traits that separate us from the careless souls who do not understand the Spirit.

As you think, so you become; your thoughts shape your reality, building castles of truth or dungeons of despair within your mind. Beware of the kingdom within you; though you believe in your righteousness, the Spirit knows all, discerning every thought and motive. Be mindful of your words, for they may condemn you. Let every thought be scrutinized before words are uttered, lest you speak death and suffer the decay of your soul. Be wary of your words. They will condemn you. Your words will not make atonement for you. Take every thought captive, as if you are a sheriff who arrests a thief to bear for a crime. Take every thought into account before a word of its translation is spoken. Better you be mute, your tongue tore out, than to speak death and reap the harvest of spoil, rot, and the decomposition of your own soul. Speak life, and life unfolds itself in ways unimagined.

I speak as one who knows the foolishness of working toward righteousness for the sake of ego. I am but a speck in the dust of all the world's dirt, a flicker of a candle's flame. Take pause when the mouth opens, and the tongue sets a field aflame."

Elwic sighed. He had heard the lesson from Magister Himself, the Sage of the Temple of Wisdom and Truth. He wondered, Have I lived up to the challenge of what I speak? Have I come close to the meaning of the words I speak? Have I embodied their meaning, or am I a hypocrite? Am I one who is a liar but proclaims a truth?

Elwic, though convicted in his heart by the words he spoke, continued. "Though you believe you reign supreme, you are foolish to believe you are righteous. The Spirit, the One whose name I dare not speak, knows the innermost parts of every thought, care, and motive you describe as holy."

The chorus of chirping crickets was a comfort. They were creatures of nature and creations of the Spirit. They sang out loud, in harmony, and on cue.

"Continue Dear Elwic. Teach of the love of Magister and His goodness!"

Elwic received the message with gladness. He cleared his throat after a sip of ale. He breathed in grace and exhaled mercy as it was given to him; Grace, the gift of breath, Mercy, the gift to continue.

"Let your actions be the evidence that claims your innocence. It is not a weakness to remain quiet. Do not babble in defense of your deeds or seek to be understood when you act from a pure heart. An obligation to explain is a selfish demand of those who need their egos caressed and eased of pain – the pain of their negligence. 'Why did you do that?' 'What were you thinking?' These are questions that do not require an answer unless you are under their authority, and even so, it does not mean you are guilty by their standard of morality.

The Spirit knows all Truth and that is what matters. When your heart is pure in your action, trust the whole of what is to come. Your name rests in the signature of a righteous letter written about you. At the end of all time, all manner of evil spoken of you will vanish. Your life is but a vapor anyway. If malice is not within, and you have taken ownership of all your actions, then rest well in the salvation of your reputation. All sins are paid for by the death of another, though you deserve the wrath; it was not commanded of you.

Therefore, if any of you say you have not sinned, you become a fool. All your works to become good are like the stinking rags that I have used to wipe my arse. Just listen! Do what is right. Seek justice. Care for the poor, the orphans, and the widows. This is the work of a pure heart! Speak when needed and listen more than you need to speak. Your ego is a weak egg. The shell is a comfort until it is cracked upon the edge of a frying pan, and your heart is heated by the fire. You wear a mask. You hide behind a wall. Likewise, you are weak until you admit your fallacy. When you take responsibility for your thoughts, your actions, and the results you get – then will you be free of condemnation and a false witness against your character? Ha! Be more offended that you have not lived a life worthy, than the words I speak that have offended you."

His words and questions probed and pricked their hearts for those who had ears to hear. To some, his words were terse and inappropriate; to others, his words caused sorrow.

He continued after a long pause.

"Let faith guide your steps, and you shall find the strength to endure."

A stranger called out. "How do I know that my faith is the guide I follow?"

"Bind these sayings around your neck. Write them on your heart. You will find favor in the sight of the Spirit and the community you inhabit. I do not speak as the author but as the lips of one who has seen Magister."

The townsfolk marveled at the promises he made, and they asked for more.

"When wisdom enters your heart and knowledge is pleasant to your soul, discretion will preserve you; understanding will keep you and deliver you from evil. For what do gold and silver do if you have no understanding of how to use them? Such is the wisdom I speak. Wisdom is gold. Understanding is silver. Though you do not see or hold wisdom and understanding in your hand, they are the cause of life, love, and treasures untold. Favor not the acquisition of riches over the attainment of wisdom. For with wisdom, all riches bow in obeisance. Riches without wisdom are fleeting shadows. As water slips through the fingers of a dreamer, so does wealth without wisdom. Many have begged for gold and silver, but they vanish from their grasp.

Service to the many provides the means to sleep in peace. Integrity and honesty in the industry are a guard against poverty. A hedge of protection is around those who honor the truth. The lies of gain by immoral means pay a dividend of destruction. Seek to be trustworthy with words, and in doing so, deeds will recompense you in multiple ways. Though you measure a seed in linear form, a seed is but the birth of vines and trees of unimaginable scope. They grow in the darkness and under the pressure of soil. The day comes to reveal the glory of their death, they rise to expand what they have sacrificed – immortality."

A weeping widow could be heard. Her cowering figure was diminished by the standing crowd. Elwic could hear the wails of a shattered heart.

"Who is the one who weeps? Bring the mourner to me."

She appeared from the dust of smoke. Her form was frail and tired. "I am here, my lord."

"Why do you weep?"

"I have no gold. I have no silver. All I have are these hands." She held them up in ransom for his word.

Elwic shook his head. "She should never weep again. Have you neglected the Widow in Havenbrook or in the town from where you have traveled? May it never be that a mother or a widow be forgotten! Come to the altar. Come to the door of the Tower and give alms to the poor and to the sustenance of the widow."

The wisdom he taught was not just for the exaltation of expression but also for the conviction of omission. And, beside the widow, a member of the crowd fell to their knees and wept to cleanse their conscience.

"When you see another in need, use your wealth for eternal gain. Is a piece of silver worth a temporary loss when used to help or heal? Is your gold more valuable than a human life? Weigh your conscience. See to it that justice and mercy is the balance of all your trade. There are those you must pass by when their palms are plump, and their bellies are full. There are also those you have ignored because your hands were plump, and your belly was full. See to it that you are aware of your heart when it is pricked to feed, to quench, or to clothe.

That is the call of the Spirit! And if you bypass the call of the Spirit, the Spirit will bypass you in your time of need. You will gasp at the tiny loss of wealth and scream, Where art thou, oh Spirit of all? Why have you forgotten me?' And the answer shall echo back from the day of your selfishness and greed, and the whisper speaks, I was here in hunger, in thirst, and in nakedness, and you fled my presence. Therefore, I flee yours. I cannot hear or see any of your pleas for help. You have received all the pleasures of life and have swallowed them into your belly. Now, you cry. Your meager suffering is pitiful. Receive the burden of your soul. Now, is the reward of those who have suffered by your negligence."

Elwic sighed. "Oh, widow of Havenbrook or be ye a traveler from afar, eat all you need, drink from the well of your family. If you are cold, there is one among us who is willing to give you a cloak."

Several members of the crowd moved forward in whispers. They sought neither reward nor fame of name but gathered around the frail frame and husked her away in quiet shame. She was the object of love, the cared-for widow, the mother of all.

She was never seen again to be crying or in want; her needs were met because of the timeless wisdom contained within the pages of The Book of Wisdom, and many would continue to learn and practice its teachings. The dark ages would be illuminated by those who sought the light in the medieval tapestry of life. Soon, the Tales of Havenbrook would spread beyond the waters and be told in a foreign tongue.

CHAPTER 16
PURITY

Shadows of wickedness loomed large over the medieval lands, where the Dark Ages made days short and the nights thick with sadness. Sickness was a precursor of death, and death was often a relief for the suffering soul. Grief became the clothing of the heart, the heavy garment of sorrow. It became a malady to the conscience, and with the cancer of death and ill of the soul, a strange disease was given birth – depravity. The culture of the day was 'live and let live, for tomorrow we die'. The brevity of life was not seen as a gift to enjoy, but rather a curse from the plague of the unknown.

'From the darkness we arise and into the same is our demise', said a Stoic traveler before he fainted in the town's square after preaching a message of doom. The townsfolk shunned his words but were obligated to bury his body free of charge. It was not an equitable trade.

And like any other time in history, there was a remnant who sought purity in a world tainted by evil. Greed was the cause of thievery; lust, the cause of seeking that which is unattainable – jealousy, fear, and envy. Why was it so difficult to find satisfaction in the breasts of one wife, or the arms of one man? There were so many errors in judgment, so many traps for the conscience to fail, and, of course, the longest-lasting enemy of a soul – the act of unforgiving another bled many dry of a pure heart.

The remnant had heard songs and tales of Elwic, the Sage of Havenbrook. They were harmonized in such a way as to promote a legend of infallible wisdom and perfect submission to the laws of nature. "He must be a god!" One lyric proclaimed. "His feet never touch the ground." (The streets of most medieval towns were filthy with the excrement of humans and animals.)

They did not know he ate fish for breakfast, and his breath was horrendous. He ate eggs for lunch, and that made for slop in his beard. His dinner was simple: a leaf of lettuce or perhaps a tasteless mashed potato with a side of beans, maybe another egg, and if he was fortunate, a slab of bacon.

Tales of heroes are laced with words that sport hollow meanings. Nevertheless, the remnant forged an alliance over time and through letters. With much planning, a meeting would take place before entering Havenbrook. An inn on the outskirts would serve the covert gathering of the remnant; The Ravenbrook Inn. From that place, the remnant would agree to be called the Ravens. It was there that they revealed to one another their identities with secret passwords and the verbiage of a cult. Once they agreed upon the day to travel into the town, they sanctified their minds with a ritual of unity – they were pure, and the rest of the world was wicked. Out of the group, one was designated as the spokesman. His name was Jahmie. That voice was the only one to ask, receive, and interrupt what the Sage would have to say. And so it was, on a dreary, rainy morning, the cobblestone streets covered in sludge mirrored the gray dingy sky as it smeared the heavens with dread, they would make their approach.

With the Tower of Havenbrook in sight, a pause was motioned by the elected leader of the Ravens, "I shall address him first, and then we shall all bow in unison." His eyes gaped for agreement, and to his surprise, the entire remnant nodded. Subordinate followers, without a backbone, bowed in servility;

they were happy to oblige. No one wanted to take the mantle of leadership without sacrifice. Jahmie, though humble in appearance with his tattered cloak and straggly, unkempt beard resembling that of a beggar, was willing to be the spokesman. In his heart, he relished the chance to be honored but kept his plea to lead silently by heaving a great sigh when elected – as though it were a heavy burden to bear. His self-righteous heart leaped with joy and relished the attention. A wet tear was forced to show his pretentious agony. "Oh, my friends, I weep for our cause."

They approached the Tower. Jahmie led the Ravens, and at the point of the group, the tip of the triangle, he raised his voice, "Dear Lord Elwic of Havenbrook, we ask for your presence to be afforded by our humble cry."

Jahmie peered over his shoulder at his followers, begging for their empathy.

Elwic appeared from the Tower. A roll of thunder punched the distant sky. A burly gray cloud bundled over the heads of all the citizens. Its appearance was ominous. A breeze dropped at rapid speed. From the sky, it pilfered through the alleys and streets with a holy vengeance – all who were within its path collapsed in obeisance to its power. Above every doorway that bore a banner of virtue, the ghostly presence whipped them into a frenzied state of chaos.

Nothing was exempt from the power. Could it be that the Magister, of The Temple of Wisdom and Truth, had returned to slay the unbelievers and mockers of his word? Rain was thick in the air. Soon it would pelt painful blows and shower the inhabitants of Havenbrook with a wave of sorrow. And then, it stopped. Was it grace, or was it a warning? The townsfolk found refuge while the Ravens stood clueless at the entrance of the Tower.

Many times, Elwic had emerged from the darkness in a calm and peaceful gait, but today - today was different. His eyes were ablaze. A grunt of dissatisfaction was heard. "Was that a snarl like a dog?" a passerby commented and then sheepishly removed themself as the Ravens tightened their ranks.

Elwic stood erect, his chest puffed out, and his nose lifted. The travelers had not asked a single question. Elwic's lips tunneled together. He breathed in deeply. A sucking wind could be heard. Air, dust, and the eyes of Havenbrook were drawn unto him. The banners of virtue leaned in toward the Tower. Saints and Sinners paused their ways. All heaven and earth stopped for a moment to ready themselves for the exhalation of Elwic. He was ready to speak, and the town of Havenbrook became quiet. Static energy was crackling. A sense of foreboding was pounding on every chest. Stillness made every heart quake – Could this be the end of all time?

The Ravens, Jahmie at the helm, stood motionless as Elwic roared.

"You have come to plead your case. You have purposed to show your sanctimonious way. I am grieved to do this again, as I have with others who come to me with a haughty heart." Elwic shook his head slightly and then began.

"You see yourself as holy, as righteous, as ones who have been tried pure in thought and deed. But I say to you now, YOU have been the filthiest of those you have condemned. Judgments placed upon the shoulders of the guilty are but linens of cloth compared to the layers of dirt and moss I see as your grave. You enter a cold tomb - your bones are dry and brittle, as is your heart.

You have caused almost irreparable damage by exposing your weakness, and you lashed out in anger. Without a gate of compromise, a storm of emotion, void of reason, watered the soil of past grievances. Misunderstandings are now given blood to beat in the heart of an enraged stallion. You came with a battered heart and a wounded soul, and with that, you attacked. As though an animal felt threatened by a perceived painful lashing, you growled, snarled, and gnashed your sharp teeth.

All logic was swallowed by self-pity and ego. You have nurtured hate when the voice of necessity bid you, 'bite the tongue!' Deafened by the bitterness in your heart, you are armed to kill. You would not listen, but instead served the sword of your tongue to cut into the flesh and bone of a perceived enemy. I know these are harsh words and likely will be dismissed as the ethereal ramblings of a stranger, but I beg of you to open the ears of your soul!

Until you have recognized the hardness of your own heart, you will be grieved and unable to forgive. And because of an unforgiving heart, your temporal body will suffer ailments that creep in without notice. Your body is a temple of the Spirit. When your spirit is not aligned with THE Spirit, there is no protection against invitational sickness and pain. You see, unforgiveness is a weapon of the Dark. The Dark makes unforgiveness seem valid. The Dark works congruently with the ego and nurtures the pain to grow. Walls and fences of unforgiveness are chains that keep your heart bound. The Dark gains power in your soul when you glorify the chains as valid, as reasonable, or as boundaries to protect you.

Ha! You have believed a lie and supported it with a claim of being righteous. You perpetuate pain; you feed it, water it, and maintain its life to extol your 'innocent soul'. Not only that but you are deceived into believing that unforgiveness is a guardian. Ha! I say it again. A lie is your belief.

Unforgiveness is not a guardian; rather, it is the master of your soul, the custodian of your mind. With it, all freedom is minimal to the point of an offense that is not worthy of eternal security. Listen to me now to save your soul. Forgiveness is a powerful tool! Though painful to employ, the capital invested reaps peace and rest beyond what could be imagined. 'Let it go!' says the Spirit. 'Take not this thought to bed.' When you share an offence with another, are you building an alliance of hatred, or are you seeking to resolve the matter?

Ha! I say it again. You have believed a lie. There is no income in sharing your offense with another, but rather poverty and a thief of joy; a debt you have taken on that has no payment to end its burden.

Your investment of words and emotion only makes the Darkness rejoice. You are so offended that if someone is not willing to defend your position, your offense is now spread like poison through the bloodstream of the community. Whispers and rumors are given birth. Suspicions and backbiting words become needles and knives into the reputation of another. The powers of words spoken with emotion are like stone walls against logic when truth scales to the top.

Ah! I say it again, you believe a lie. Everything spoken, whether in truth or a lie, has power. Choose wisely and live – choose carelessly and die.

Sow the seeds of empathy and understanding among any adversary. As you sow, so you shall reap. You claim to seek purity, and yet, you hold another ransom for sins that you have committed in secret. You have failed the very mantra you preach. Furthermore, you wish not for purity! You wish that others be brought to shame!"

The Ravens were demolished. They cowered. They crumbled. Jahmie dared not look over his shoulder to see his clan. He knew the words of Elwic were true, and he was the worst of all. His heart trembled in fear. His hands began to shake at his side. The man's skin rippled with waves of conviction. He was alone. All sin was exposed. The darkness of his heart was exposed by beautiful light – the words of truth.

All selfish expectations he had placed on someone else's shoulders were vaporized by the power of the Sage's words. He had judged all others with purity based solely on his idea of justice and honor. His ways were not the ways of the higher One.

Elwic sighed three times. His temperament moderated with each cleansing breath. One breath in – the Ravens dropped to their knees in repentance. They were pulled to the dirt and fell, prostrate, before the Tower. Powerless and made transparent; their hearts were far from being pure, and their minds were given to the logic of emotion – that terrifying evil that binds a soul without escape.

One breath out - they wheezed and wept aloud while begging for mercy and forgiveness. The whimpers of the travelers followed. They were weakened by the authority of the words of which they thought they had commanded. And then the rocks from the ground shimmered to the surface and gave out an utterance; a language none could understand. Never had the stones, buried deep in the earth's grave, revealed themselves without the gritty plow of a sweaty farmer. The stones and their greater siblings, the rocks, joined in a chorus of sound that outperformed the proud voices of any heart.

The second breath in – Elwic placed his arms out to his side to give his lungs the space to expand. He sucked in deep. The banners of Havenbrook stretched their tattered threads toward his presence. Symbols of virtue praised the air that called them forward. The banners of Havenbrook bowed in reverence at the breath of the one who knew the Spirit and spoke the ancient language of Truth.

The second breath out – the impending storm of thunder, lightning, and rain gave up its threat and spread thin as a fog into the distance. They were chased by a wind hurled at them with a force no man or woman had ever seen. The banners weathered the blast and then dropped lifeless; they hung from their poles without motion; honored to be a material subject to the breath of one who knew the Spirit.

The third breath in – The Earth itself began to shake; mountains that stood guard on either side of Havenbrook began to dissolve and fall to pieces. The trees that sustained the town with shelter, warmth, and safety uprooted all at once, and at that great collapse, pointed their tops toward the Tower; the roots became exposed to the elements. Trembling to their core, the trees gave total obeisance to the voice that had called them to be - from seed to their final form.

The third breath out - The sound of rushing water poured from Elwic's mouth. It could not be seen but was felt as a violent twisting and turning of fate. None could resist the force. Whisked about like rags being churned in a barrel of hot water and lye, the entire inhabitants of Havenbrook were swallowed and drowned in the vengeance and holiness of the breath; the hot and mournful breath of one sent by Magister himself.

And then, utter silence. Not a chirp of any bird was heard. The townsfolk blinked from their places of refuge. They had not drowned and been taken to the afterlife. The air above the town flirted with the wisps of smoke from the chimneys. The mountains were back in place in their strong station and verdantly guarded the town. The trees were gathered and raised their greenery toward the sun. They were redeemed to stand again and be the majestic providers assigned to them as they had been promised. The banners of virtue flapped in gaiety as if a dream brought them rest and the courage to continue.

"You will never be righteous!" Elwic's voice resounded. "When your mortal mind believes it to be true, you have placed a nail in your flesh, and then another, and then one more. All your thinking is rags, a pile of dung. And with it, you approach me in false pretense! You want me to side with you – to take up your offense. Ha! You have believed a lie. Only Magister has shown the perfect way. You will go from here and leave your piety at the bonfire. It will be burned, and the ashes of it forgotten. You will go from here and take with you the fruit of forgiveness. You have received it without cost or sacrifice, and thus, you shall honor the gift you have received and share it with others without cost or sacrifice."

Jahmie was ashamed of his thoughts, his actions, and the results they had birthed.

Elwic knew the consciousness of the Raven leader was prodded and pricked to the core.

"Jahmie, many will come to the Temple of Wisdom and Truth with reprobate minds. Many will come to plead their case of self-righteousness. Many will proclaim their rights and justifications, but all will fail because the mortal mind is a temporary disease until made clean by the eternal wisdom of Magister."

Elwic lowered his arms to his side. Jahmie glanced up from

his tear-stained cheeks. "I am one relieved of his riches, a pauper at the feet of a master. Forgive me for my indolence, my judgmental heart, and oh Lord Elwic, forgive me for my pride! For I thought I was right when believing I was the pure one and the other one the wicked."

"Jahmie, purity comes when forgiveness is for all. The anger and wrath of all that is right fall upon us when one believes that your right comes before all right. The act of forgiveness is not merely an external gesture, but a profound internal transformation that liberates individuals from the burden of resentment and animosity, and with that liberty creates a peaceful heart, tranquil in all its ways." Elwic paused and looked at Jahmie, "You do want peace and well-being, don't you?"

"Oh yes! Yes, my lord!"

"Well then, from now on, do not avoid the darkness that surrounds you but confront it with unwavering goodness and grace. Before today, you have cast aside disagreements as though they were dark words in your world of light. From this day on, when your piety comes to your mind, cast it aside as the evil cloak it is. From this day on, see to it that grace and forgiveness are your first defense so that purity is the water that cleanses the offense. As the blacksmith of any village can teach you – when the hardness of metal is heated, it can be cleansed and shaped. In the forge of your heart, temper the steel of your resolve with compassion, kindness, and selflessness. Let these virtues be the quenching waters that cleanse the impurities of the world, but not of your own strength, so you may boast that it is from your heart; rather, you boast because of Magister, the Sage of The Temple of Wisdom and Truth who taught you.

Though I am a mediator, a spokesman, and the firstborn from the Temple, you also are the light because you have shared the wick with me. And when you return from where you have come, keep the words I speak in your heart. To find purity, you must be a beacon of light in the darkest of nights. Stand firm in the face of adversity when you wish to make yourself righteous, and let your actions speak louder than any words. Extend the forgiveness you have received, and purity will be yours! Your deeds will be the seeds that bear the fruit of purity."

The Ravens gathered themselves together and made haste into the world outside the Town of Havenbrook. Each of them became troubadours of purity, bathing themselves in the word of the master. And so, their words, deeds, and lives became echoes and ripples that began at The Temple of Wisdom and Truth and were proclaimed to them by Elwic, the Sage of Havenbrook.

I write these words and lay them down with ink and quill so the lessons may be inscribed on your heart, say I, Actar, the scribe of Havenbrook.

CHAPTER 17

THE KING IS COMING

The Celebration of Havenbrook was in seven days. Each year, the villagers looked forward to the grand event to remember the birth of the Tower of Havenbrook. Its reputation, though slow in momentum, had built to a fever pitch in the ears of surrounding hamlets, villages, towns, and even the King of Avaloria. Rumors were percolating that the King himself would make the journey to visit the birthplace of the Tower where Elwic, the Sage of Havenbrook, placed every log, hewn by his father, to construct a place of education that brought the knowledge from the Temple of Wisdom and Truth to an earthly kingdom.

In preparation for the chance honor that the King would pare a slice of his time to visit, the cloth makers of Havenbrook were busy weaving tapestries of oral tales into visual displays for mortal minds to remember. The town of Havenbrook hummed with a vibrancy of expectation. Whispers of joy and delight, at times, exploded into an unexplained cacophony of laughter and a few lungs wheezing for breath. At any other time, a passer-by in the marketplace may have easily been perturbed by the interruption of noise - but the spirit in the air was one of forgiveness, grace, and expectancy. An unusual event was to occur, and, in the short lifetimes of village folk, the event was a once-in-a-lifetime celebration.

A mysterious minstrel appeared during a day of preparation and sang a prayer, a tune of repentance. None knew from where he came, but his words struck fear in their hearts.

"The King is coming! Let us prepare our domiciles with decorations of life. Let us prepare our hearts and be pure of the sins of pride, jealousy, and avarice. The King is coming! Our ways are like a worm whose belly pushes the dirt aside to travel in vain. His way, the King's way, is higher, nobler, and shall ever be the light to which we long to be. May He find us obedient to the words He speaks and understand the calling He grants us to fulfill."

One did not need to be part of the inner circle to receive His care. However, the chapels became weak in understanding what the King meant when he gave His words to the scribes. The interpretation was skewed to mean: 'If one does not faithfully attend or tithe to the local chapel, an expression of the King's love and care, one risks becoming lost to the world's travails and trials. Therefore, seek the counsel of the resident monk and the servants of the chapel, and then shall your needs be met when you are sick and thirsty, without clothing, in prison, and without a home.'

The least of all men were forgotten, shunned, or neglected because they were not part of the sanctioned plan of membership in the local expression of the King's chapel.

Much of the early scrolls were written to free all from the treachery of guilt, shame, and constant unforgiveness, but as the monks soon realized, with freedom comes the expression of free will, and THAT was dangerous. Free will meant independent thinking – thinking without constraint. Ideas could flourish to be an eventual breaking-of-chains from the rules and implicit desires of the chapel. An agreement was forged among the cabal of monks. They would control access to the scrolls. Only elected teachers were deemed worthy of the existential wisdom hidden deep within the papyrus. All others were deemed unworthy;

their sin, ever before them, was a stain on the purity of holiness ascribed to the scrolls.

Incremental steps to give proof-of-faith became layers of rules, and each set became more difficult to attain. Little by little, the people felt unworthy – the summit of holiness was unattainable. The self-righteous monks offered promises to those who understood and accepted their lowly state – "offer up a tenth of all you have and sacrificial alms. In return, you will receive a harvest from your seed. Do not lend to the poor before you have given your dues to the chapel, and we will see to it that those who deserve the care of the chapel will receive it."

These requirements crushed the purity of hearts, the somber souls, and the seekers of sanctification for those who were lost without a voice. To be cared for was contingent on a degree of attendance and the gifts one gave.

The King was saddened by the rules that gripped and bound his constituents. He wanted them to be free. He had heard of the Sage of Havenbrook. He had heard how the hamlet had grown into a village and now a prosperous town, in large part because of a teacher who, in earnest faith, brought the teachings from the Temple of Wisdom and Truth and gave them freely to the poor without cost or expectation of recompense. He was pleased to hear that the Spirit was alive and sought after.

A messenger was sent from the castle of Avaloria to the town of Havenbrook. He arrived dressed in the most vibrant shades of purple - plum, sangria, magenta, and mulberry. The coif about his head was the lightest color, magenta, bordered in plum. Flowing from his shoulders was mulberry, followed by a tunic dyed in sangria—perfectly resembling a grape's different tastes and plumpness! Though his garb could entice a guffaw of laughter, his presence was regarded as a harbinger of royalty. None would dare breathe the disrespectful tongue of merriment; rather, they leaned into the gift of the messenger as though he were a footstool for the feet of a master.

"The King is coming! He will be attending the celebration.

May He find us obedient to His words and understand the calling he grants us to fulfill."

The messenger then sought refuge in an alehouse. He collapsed after too many drinks made accessible by the welcoming patrons of Havenbrook. And why shouldn't the gifts of the citizenry be showered upon him?

All doubt was cast aside at his ability to use his tongue. He was dressed in the regalia of the King's court. Indeed, he would speak kindly and seek favors from the king himself. Indeed, he would remember his benefactors' names as they slapped his back and praised him for his selfless service to their king! A jester's song was born at the event, and its tune was sung many years later.

Drunken minds are vacant of memory,
and the drink's aroma is want of flavor.
Without the light of thought and reason,
each giver and receiver is a fount of treason.
Though the tongue is blessed with momentary pleasure,
the lips are cursed to offer temporary treasure.
Thus, the lesson is learned and earned.
Sanctify the mind and eye until thy word is honored on high.
When the senses were dulled, the tongue grew sharp,
and the wits were dim.

The herald spoke aloud, then sank away from his duty.

The Town of Havenbrook breathed, ate, and drank in the joy that the grandest of all, the King of Avaloria, would be taking part in the anniversary of the Tower. Many merchants upgraded the care of their wares, shining the brass and silver linings to impress the ONE who gave them license to live within the kingdom's boundaries. Without a thought of frugality or the loss of profit on the morrow, many of the tradesmen and shopkeepers poured their meager earnings into fresh banners and signs to impress the King. Proper dressings were purchased to impress the royal crew, some of which none had ever seen.

Even the goats of Sirion, Ja and Neen, formerly called Meek and Mo, were paraded for days ahead of the celebration. The beasts were covered with cloths of purple, and the bells that hung around their necks were burnished to shine like copper – all a show to impress the townsfolk of Havenbrook. And with a chorus of laughter and hilarity, the townsfolk enjoyed watching the goats as they rolled about and soiled the royal coats with the droppings of their own disgusting dung. The dereliction of their duty to remain loyal to a pompous and piteous appearance caused Sirion much distress. As the pointed fingers and cackles subsided, Sirion took them home for a thorough wash in a creek on the edge of town.

His goats would return to the state they were meant for— naked and bare as they were born and naked and bare as they would die. Colored garments are nothing more than veils, hiding both the body and the soul inside. Masks, the desperate attempt to be what one was never meant to be.

"Dear Elwic!" A citizen of Havenbrook scurried by the tower. "Are we ready? Have we proven to be worthy of such great honor, to have the King of Avaloria grace the streets and shops of Havenbrook?"

Elwic's eyes crinkled. "There is nothing you could do to impress or depress his love for you. You scamper about and shake in fear when the One who has known you from afar now sees the flesh that covers the soul. It is all in vain."

The feverish citizen's ears were like hollow straws of hay— words entered one side and tumbled out the other, falling to the scuffled dirt below. A puff of dust was the only trace that words had been spoken, but none had taken root in the frazzled mind of the passerby. As the particles settled, the citizen, burdened with needless worries, hurried off, still lacking the cure of a peaceful heart. Elwic observed the outlandish attention paid to outward appearances—a glaring disadvantage to both heart and soul. Starving for vision and lost in an ego-driven circus of colors and costumes, the townsfolk were trapped in a shallow game of masks.

Elwic could not address them all individually, and the nightly bonfires were not being attended since the announcement was made – The King is Coming! So, he sighed and entered a rest for a long nights' sleep.

A veil of fog lay low over Havenbrook. As though a blanket had kept the merchants, the tradesmen, the artisans, the shopkeepers, and the farmers warm and sleepy, a woman and her husband stumbled into town. Their baby cried from the wrappings and awakened the glassmaker. He crept to his door and peered through the hole. He pressed his eyes hard and then opened them again. "Are you lost at this hour?" He spoke as he opened his door.

They swayed their heads. "Nay! We seek shelter. The King is coming!"

The glassmaker snorted, "The King has not arrived yet! You are waking me, and I need my rest. I will greet him when I am awake and ready. Be gone! Find an alley or a stable to wait until morning."

He closed the door and found his bed. The drift into dreams was welcome, though tinged with guilt, eased only by the thought that the latecomers were merely irresponsible travelers.

The daylight came, and the drowsy town stirred from slumber. Embers were stoked to ignite fresh wood. Early morning grunts were exchanged as the shopkeepers threw out their urine and gasped at the odor of their neighbors' dung.

Curls of morning breaths were swirling from all the animals as they stirred from their hay to greet the day. The first murmurs of complaints were always from the cows.

A young boy darted to and fro across the cobblestones. He was scrambling for a crust, a peel of fruit, or perhaps a small potato cast aside by a plump merchant.

"Alms for the poor. Alms for the poor." A beggar's voice pierced the morning chatter.

"Another beggar?" A shopkeeper barked angrily at his neighbor, the potter.

The potter replied, "The King is coming! And with him, the

poor and the wretched, the hungry, the thirsty, and the naked. It's to be expected—they're always near when the King passes, especially for those of us who have earned the harvest!"

"Looking for a handout, I am sure. Why do they bother?" The shopkeeper jeered.

The beggar came closer and veered to the widest cobblestone street where the most prosperous merchants held their business. The banners of virtue hung limp, heavy from the morning dew. The banners appeared to be mourning as well, as if a forbearance of mood was in collusion with the dawn - that is, the ignorance and chastisement of the poor.

"Alms for the poor." The voice rang out again.

The shopkeeper winked at the potter, "Here we are! Come see us!"

Within a moment, a figure emerged from the wispy fog and floated above the polished stones of the street. A ghost! The first thought of the potter as he inhaled but soon released his hot breath into the cold morning air. The shopkeeper next door let out the first curse, "Havenbrook is not for you. Be gone!"

The translucent figure bowed away and veered toward another path in the town.

"Ha! That's all it took, potter! One harsh word and off the beggar went!"

The two collaborated in laughter.

"Alms for the poor." The figure's voice echoed. Another shopkeeper joined in solidarity and threw out a worded jab, "We are preparing for the King, not a vagabond or ethereal Thing! Be gone!"

Down the narrow street, the potter and the glassmaker heard the verbal swipe and forced out a laugh from a distance with the intent to be heard. Of course, it sounded unnatural and insincere, but it was granted acceptance as a collaborative agreement.

No one wanted the streets of Havenbrook to be crowded with the poor, the hungry, and the beggars on the eve of the coming of their King. They thought too much effort was given to paint the town with beauty and energy to be thwarted by the grim reality of what has been, what is, and what will be – "the poor will be with you always." Oh, that dastardly truth!

Elwic was troubled when he heard the rumors of his beloved townsfolk being careless with their words. Words – the means of moving the hearts and minds of his world to be free from the tyranny of bondage – and yet, words were the weapons waged in a war of sabotage! He was disgusted and tore his tunic in anger. He made his way to the square of Havenbrook; his ragged appearance caught the attention of the town. Not long would he speak and declare at the ninth hour of the day – "The King is coming? The King has Come and You have received Him not! He is in the smolder of flames, the stench of your deeds, and He is about the redemption of your sins! There He is!"

The townspeople gathered closer, shuffling into a crowd. 'Where? Where?" Voices rippled out.

Elwic's eyes widened. "See that beggar!" He shouted. Spit shot from his mouth. "He is why the King cometh! He is why we all bear the fruit of the Tower, the teachings of the Temple of Wisdom and Truth! The King is coming to see the fruition of our deeds. But we have covered Havenbrook with flags, banners, and symbols of virtues, and yet we have laughed at the root of our cause. We have shamed ourselves. We have prepared a curtain that hides the stage from which we perform. Don't you see? Your weakness to appear holy is a veil of your own ego. Filthy rags! That's what you show the King!

Each one of you has met him and you are unaware. And in your ignorance, he sees the shallow silks and the see-through shades you call a glorified work. He laughs at your offering and weeps at the effect of your effort. The wall of your heart is braced for strength, but the soul of his Kingdom is a river, a fountain of life, a bath of cleansing. Lay down the bricks of your boldness. Set aside the whims of your wanting. See the greater good outside the boundaries of your own brooding to be the best of the best. See not the glory of your gain but rather the bastion of your beliefs and repent from it, for you have violated the covenant of love, compassion, and the will of all that is pure. Live the purpose of your calling and share the bounty with all!"

Elwic leaned forward as if to faint. He caught his breath and spoke again.

"That beggar who screams, that figure in the fog, 'Alms for the poor' is but an example of what we are, who we are, and why we are!!! Don't you see? The beggar is WHY the King is coming and has come!"

The crowd of listeners fell prostrate. Weeping and wailing became waves of an emotional currency; a monetary pulse of value that changed the hearts of Havenbrook.

The beggar turned toward the cacophony of travail. His eyes made haste and were captive to the platform of Elwic. A mysterious cumulus cloud descended from the heavens and enshrouded the 'alms for the poor' messenger. It carried him to the square where Elwic stood – The Sage of Havenbrook with his tunic torn, his eyes welling with tears, and from his mouth panted wisps of fleeting breaths.

The carrier cloud lowered the stranger just behind the Sage. His height was more pronounced as he towered over Elwic. A momentary reprieve in grief was sanctioned as the beggar began to disrobe his tattered rags. The sun broke through the firmament and blasted rays of light, illuminating the creature that now stood like a statue; an omnipotent creature wearing the most royal garb of a King. Purple extended from his person in ripples, as though carried in ethereal songs of light and purity.

Elwic turned his head to see the glory behind him and fell to his knees, throwing himself away from the presence of His master. A breathless silence was followed by an eruption of moans and deep-seated mourning; a language none could understand.

"My children," A silken voice rolled and rumbled out with the same measure of authority and compassion. The frequency of the sound caressed the mourners.

"I have seen your deeds and the souls of Havenbrook. You have made a home and fortune from the seeds and fruit of the earth I have given you. Some have been grateful, and some have been hateful. Today is not the judgment of all deeds. Today is the challenge to be aware of those who cross the path you trod. Though you are granted the breath of life, death is the ever-present victor of all. Time is the mocker of all expectations. No power is greater than the marker of time, except the power of love.

Love is the truest of all expressions. It explains itself in acts of trust, forgiveness, sacrifice, and an uncommon belief when all evidence fights for the contrary. Doubt is the enemy of your soul. Fear is a selfish miser that robs you. Hate is the thief that will kill you. Vanity is a deceiver. Ego is a liar. Pride will blind you. Envy causes laziness. Lust perverts the goodness of love. And greed, greed, will separate you from the glorious power of unity. The heart of greed sacrifices life and dies alone, and all the riches are squandered by animals of thirst and hunger.

But alas! You can have redemption if you listen with your heart beyond hearing the word with your ears. Do not be tempted to believe the senses of your mortal coil. They have lied when your eyes glance away from truth, when whispers of gossip are heard, and when the taste of wine thickens the mind. Rather, be sober, able to discern the wicked and the thief you have allowed in the temple of your soul. You speak that you have love for truth, but your heart is far from it."

The people sobbed until their throats were dry. They gasped for water. As sure as his words made them parched and sad, his next proclamations gave them hope, and began to quench their thirst and dry their tears.

"Seek justice, so your soul will rest in peace. Act in chastity so you may be regarded as pure. Offer charity so you will prosper. Be patient and offer forgiveness as it will be measured and meted back upon you. Use kindness as a tool to build your community. Understand humility, as you have fallen short of all that is good. Be diligent in all you do so that your fruit will grow. And may temperance be a guide for your daily intakes – your love of food, of luxury, of arrogance, of pride, and any excess that is not worthy of your reputation – keep watch as the eye and the stomach hunger more than the soul.

My children! Your righteous acts are the evidence to those who walk through this land and that I am your King, your ruler, and most importantly, your father."

With that, the figure in the mist, the beggar, the King, the messenger to the souls in Havenbrook bade them a farewell salutation. "I am Magister, and I love you!"

A breeze fluttered softly, and soon the sound of the wind could be heard. Nearby, a flock of birds took flight, and the banners of virtues flapped in applause. Havenbrook began to shake. Shingles on rooftops became restless and clamored to their demise on the cobblestone streets.

Another wind howled from a distance, sweeping through the narrow streets like a whirlwind, causing the loose stones of every shack, shanty, and shop to cry out. Magister smiled. A stratus cloud swooped in, harmonizing with the rushing sound of the wind, and gathered the beggar, who was the King, lifting him to a place above the town. He hovered in a miraculous form.

All eyes could see him. They saw his pain and mourned. Every mouth bled with words of praise and adoration for the King who lowered himself into the flesh of the lowliest. He did not arrive in pomp and glory; rather, his entrance was meek and humble. He did not proclaim his power but showed his authority through his words. Surely, his anger could have slain the wickedness of his mockers, but he showed compassion and received the disdain of his earthly cloak. Surely, he could have demanded the respect of his throne, but instead, he allowed the hearts of the town to be exposed to what they had become. His light made their souls' shadows appear as they turned away from him. His light exposed all they tried to hide, even when they turned their backs on his beauty.

And then he vanished into the sky, and the town of Havenbrook heaved in sorrow and mourned with heavy hearts.

Elwic wept. The threads of his tightly woven earthly cloth,

his mind, and his way of thinking were all tattered, crushed, and shattered by the presence of Magister. He had forgotten that he was a piece of clay – a pliable, pitiful piece of a puzzle in the play of an eternal timeline.

Elwic was a servant, a silent contributor to the spectrum of what was destined to be from the beginning of time. He was the beloved son, the daughter, the father, and the mother of all he would touch and speak to. Elwic was a name, an identity that was given, a gift to the world. He was to be the son of a King, the model of his father, and the messenger of a higher calling. His life was a vessel of the higher spirit, the King of Avaloria– the voice of Magister.

His life was a temporary glance for all to see what Magister would reveal. The more he opened his heart to the teachings of the ancient sage, the more he emptied himself of control over himself. He was a mouthpiece, a prophet, and the wick of God; a flame that faintly flickered. As all mortals would be, a whisper barely heard among the shouts of all time, Elwic, the wick of God, spoke louder but was ashamed that his ego was also heard.

The potter and the glassmaker repented of their evil ways. They saw the peril of their hearts' intent when chastising the lost and poor in the world, and those who wandered into the town of Havenbrook looking for help. All they had was the gift of language and the power of their tongues, and they gambled with it in the foolish mockery of a beggar.

The beggar was the King!

What an imprudent use of their lips and the gift of reason. From that day forward, all who entered the boundaries of Havenbrook were seen as a representation of the King and treated as such.

The lesson was learned - those who entertain the lowest of beings may be entering into communion with the spirit of the King. The lesson was never forgotten. The King was present in every soul. Whether the townsfolk thought it worthy to judge or not, a new creed of generosity was birthed in the hearts of all. Every living thing could and would be respected and honored as though the King himself were venturing across their path. It was a challenge, as lower souls would take advantage of kindness and compassion. But as the creed was taught – Better you be judged for giving to the wrong person than be judged for not giving at all.

Havenbrook became known as the Haven of Souls. It was a place where the King was honored and understood. It was a village of people who held their expectations hostage until objective witnesses were given a proper audience and biases were on trial for authenticity.

Elwic was now a vacant vessel to be filled with nothing but the King's word, his spirit, and the calling he was to fulfill for the sake of his King.

And, as any tale would do, it would lead to the next adventure of hope, of the development of courage, and the strengthening of character – but only IF one can see life as a temporary glimpse of eternity. Elwic leaned in and, with his eyes closed, waited to hear the voice of Magister. And then … it happened.

CHAPTER 18

THE BID TO COME

"PEOPLE WHO HOLD THE TRUTH WITHIN THEIR HEARTS NEVER NEED to raise a defense. People who believe a lie need the force of an army to defend the walls they have built. Seek to be without guile. Know that when you are ready to speak, your words are formed by the spirit of innocence but carry the menace of a dragon."

Elwic recalled the words of the Magister from the Temple of Wisdom and Truth. The memories of his time spent learning at the sage's feet often came to him in dreams. Upon waking, he would record the ancient teachings, transforming them into a curriculum for the Tower.

On a late afternoon, Elwic stood at the edge of the Tower's highest parapet, gazing out over the vast expanse of the land. The sun was setting, casting a golden hue over the fields and forests below. The town of Havenbrook had seen a productive day of trade and the advancement of knowledge. The flags that paraded the streets, hoisted in place above every shop of commerce, symbols of virtue, were being rolled up and placed away with care.

In the distance, he could see a fog as it lilted over the area where the Temple of Wisdom and Truth was purported to be;

that sacred place where he sacrificed his youth to become a scholar of Magister.

It had been many years since he had left the simple life of a farmer's son to seek knowledge and wisdom at the Temple. The journey had been long and arduous, but it had been worth every step. The teachings of the Magister had transformed him, filling his heart with a profound sense of purpose and clarity.

As the sky darkened, Elwic descended the winding stairs of the Tower, the words of the Magister echoing in his mind. The Tower was quiet, its halls empty save for the occasional flicker of torchlight. It was a place of solitude and reflection, where students, scholars, and sages came to study and contemplate the mysteries of the universe.

Elwic entered his study chamber, a small but comfortable room filled with books and scrolls. He sat at his desk, lighting a candle and pulling out a fresh sheet of parchment. As he dipped his quill into the ink, he closed his eyes, allowing the memories of his time at the Temple to wash over him.

Magister had been a towering figure, both physically and intellectually. His eyes, sharp and penetrating, seemed to see into the very soul of those who stood before him. Elwic could still remember the day he had first arrived at the Temple, a young and eager student hungry for knowledge. Magister had welcomed him with a kind smile after testing him – would he feed a hungry old man or leave him to die? But it had not taken long for Elwic to realize that the path to wisdom would be far from easy.

The lessons had been rigorous, challenging not just his intellect but his very character. Magister had taught that true wisdom was not merely the accumulation of knowledge, but the understanding and application of that knowledge in the pursuit of truth and justice.

"People who hold the truth within their hearts never need to raise a defense," Magister had said. "For the truth is its own defense, unassailable and eternal. And those who spew and

believe a lie need an army to defend the walls they have built."
The words echoed again and again in his mind.

Elwic had taken those words to heart, striving to live by
them in all his endeavors. It had not always been easy. There
had been times when he had been tempted to take the easy path,
to bend the truth for the sake of convenience or personal gain.
But he had always remembered Magister's teachings, and it had
given him the strength to stay true to his principles.

As he wrote, Elwic felt a deep sense of peace and fulfillment.
The ancient teachings flowed effortlessly from his pen, each
word a tribute to the wisdom of Magister. He knew that the
curriculum he was creating would guide future generations of
scholars, ensuring that the light of truth would continue to shine
brightly in the world – after he was gone.

Amid his writing, a soft knock at the door interrupted his
thoughts. It was his faithful scribe, Actar. Elwic smiled,
accustomed to the playful and rhythmic knocks Actar would
drum on any door, a signature of his cheerful nature.

"Anika came to warn of a stranger in town asking about the
whereabouts of the Tower and of you, my Lord!"

Elwic carefully placed his quill on the side of the parchment.
"She is concerned."

"Lord," Actar said, tilting his head at the oddity. "It is past
dusk. She wasn't carrying a lamp. I fear she was frightened,
keeping her warning just for us and her movements secret."

Elwic glanced at the parchments and sighed. "I am not
finished yet."

"Lord?"

"Actar, you have faithfully recorded my words, but I am
compelled to write down the teachings the Magister has
entrusted to me. My task is not yet complete, and the day is
coming..." Elwic paused, aware that his next words would
weigh heavily on his devoted disciple.

"Lord?" Actar's voice was tinged with concern.

Elwic sensed Actar's anxiety and began a private lesson.
"There once was a King who sought the meaning of life, of

death, planting, and harvest. His ancient words still resonate. Everything has its season, Actar. There is a time to kill and a time to heal, a time to tear down and a time to build. A time to weep and a time to laugh; a time to mourn and a time to dance. A time to lose and a time to gain. Thus, understanding his wisdom can illuminate the ways of everything under the sun, where nothing is truly new."

Actar's mouth fell open, and his heart clenched with fear. "What are you saying, Lord Elwic? I am troubled by your words." He panted for breath.

Elwic stood and approached Actar, extending his arms for an embrace. "All things must end for new things to begin."

The two men hugged, and Actar struggled to hold back his tears. Elwic's presence was comforting, and Actar inhaled the rich, deep scent of incense lingering on his master's robes, knowing this might be the last time he would be so close.

Elwic gently released Actar and placed his hands on his shoulders, tightening his grip until Actar raised his head from his tears. "Go, Actar. Let us open the door for the stranger."

Drops of rain pelted the compressed dirt just outside the Tower's door. A figure approached, clad in a dark, hooded robe. The stranger moved forward with an ethereal grace, his presence both serene and commanding attention.

Curious as always, and never afraid to ask, Elwic beckoned the creature to uncloak his face.

"Who are you?"

The streams of water shimmered as the figure came closer. Elwic stood firm.

"You must be drenched, and I bid you come, but you must reveal your face."

The voice of the traveler spoke, "I am a monk and seek shelter from this storm."

Elwic shook his head. The storm had started before the sun had set, and surely this monk was lost, or was he? He did ask Anika for directions to the Tower, and he was marching in a straight line. Elwic decided he would give him refuge; after the storm passed and a good night's rest, he would bid him well.

"Come in, traveler. We have vittles and grog to warm your stomach and a fire to dry your body." He nodded at the hooded guest as he floated by.

The crackling fire, though barely a flame, gave the warmth and comfort the monk needed. Rubbing his hands and welcoming the heat, he giggled and then began to laugh.

"Are you Elwic, the Sage of Havenbrook?"

Elwic was startled by the question.

"I am." He furrowed his brow.

The monk was younger than most. His curly black locks resembled those of a cherub with dark hair.

"Elwic," the monk's voice was a whisper on the wind, ancient and knowing. "Your journey here is complete, and your destiny calls you beyond these hills, beyond the rich soil that you have cultivated."

Elwic turned, his eyes meeting those of the monk. There was something in those eyes—a depth of wisdom and a hint of sorrow—that spoke of distant lands and uncharted paths. But he was shocked at the words: "Your journey here is complete, and your destiny calls you beyond these hills, beyond the rich soil that you have cultivated."

"What?" Elwic asked.

The monk smiled, rubbing his hands together and blowing out a breath. "I knew this would be your first response. I was afraid to make the case, but HE sent me."

Elwic leaned in toward the monk. The seats, crafted from logs forged by his father's hands, were now worn by decades of students, disciples, guests, and seekers of wisdom who had fidgeted back and forth. "HE?" Elwic sat upright. "When you say HE, I only know of one name that comes to mind, and..." Elwic thought, perhaps I should test the monk.

"I have a name in mind. If you speak the name, then I know you come in honor and in truth. What is the name of HE?"

The monk lifted his eyes from the fire. "His name is Magister, and he speaks highly of you."

Chills ran down Elwic's spine. "You have met Magister?"

A giggle escaped the monk's mouth. "Oh yes! I was a traveler seeking the wisdom of ages when I stumbled upon a beggar…"

Elwic interrupted, "It was Magister, wasn't it, the beggar you met?"

The monk laughed. "Yes, oh yes, it was! He was endearing, charming, and quite the talker. He invited me to his camp. I did not know he was the ONE I was looking for. I thought I was helping a beggar, and here HE was, the King of my heart." The monk laughed again; his teeth shone with the brilliance of complete truth. "I met the ONE I was seeking when I served the least of all creation."

Elwic trembled. "Have you been…" he dared not ask the question. "Have you been to…" He paused again. That sacred memory of his youth was on his lips, that place of holiness, that time of water, of the raven, that place in the Spirit of time that mortal man scarcely knows, save for a few who venture with the purity of a child. Summoning courage, he finally spoke the words.

"Have you been to The Temple of Wisdom and Truth?" Elwic almost fainted at his own question, his heart stuttered.

Time slowed to a crawl. The flames did not flicker. The flames curled in such a way that one could reach in and grab a coal without the threat of a burn. The wisps of smoke turned about in curiosity, questioning their role in the space they inhabited for the moment.

The monk slowly turned his stare from the embers embedded at the soul of the fire and spoke. "I have."

"One thing I ask," Elwic stated. "When you were in the Temple, did you know the raven?"

The monk nodded his head. "You mean the black bird who ate his fill every day?" He laughed. "Yes, and he ate some of my portion too!"

Elwic gasped and wept. "Yes. He was my friend, my guide, and…" Elwic had to pause to catch his breath as his heart seemed to skip a beat. That raven was the memory of his youth, the curse and the cure on his journey to the Temple of Wisdom and Truth. "And is he alive?"

"He is alive and well, I assure you." The monk beamed.

The words were a comfort, as the bird of prey would have been three decades old, if not more. Pleased with the answer, Elwic asked, "Why me? Why does Magister seek an audience with me through you?" His voice was steady, though his mind raced with questions. "Why are you here? What is it you want of me?"

"Because you are chosen," the monk replied. "There is a greater purpose that awaits you, one that can only be fulfilled if you leave behind all that you have known."

As the monk's words lingered in the air, Elwic felt a pull, an undeniable call to adventure and discovery. He stood quickly and ran to the door of the Temple. It swung open without a hand upon its heavy door. The rain had stopped, and an eerie moonlit sky illuminated the town. The moon's light bathed the town in a glorious glow. Elwic's heart melted with love and gratitude. The village of Havenbrook had grown into a town, a place of bustling commerce and spiritual growth. The village of his birth, now a town, had given him a new life since his return from the Temple of Wisdom and Truth and the heartbreaking death of his beloved father. But the call forward to a new horizon beckoned him. The unknown beckoned with promises of mystery and revelation. His faith could be made stronger in the presence of his mentor, the Spirit of Magister.

With a heavy yet resolute heart, Elwic turned from the door, his eyes locked with the monks; he nodded. "I will go."

The monk smiled, a gesture filled with both encouragement and respect. "Then follow me, Elwic of Havenbrook. The world awaits your arrival."

The night swallowed the three souls. Elwic collapsed in a pile of rugs and furs, Actar led the monk to a room to find rest, and he, the faithful scribe of Elwic for many years, found his room vacant and meaningless as he longed for a yesterday before the monk of the future had arrived.

The next morning arrived abruptly, offering little respite to the restless souls. The monk questioned the reach of his influence. Elwic awoke with a flicker of fear, while Actar felt the weight of loneliness as he pondered his role as a scribe—uninvited by the monk to journey where Elwic was called. He questioned his value, his worth, and his future, wondering how one man's word could determine the fate of another.

"A breakfast, lord?" Actar motioned his hands toward the embers that roasted a potato.

"Actar, my faithful one. I will have breakfast with you. The tuber of the earth will be our gift to each other."

The monk watched in admiration. The sage of Havenbrook and his scribe barely spoke a word as they chewed and swallowed. Their playful eye contact spoke volumes without a sound. They nodded at each other. Actar's eyes welled with tears. Elwic bowed his head. The moment was thick with emotion. Neither knew what to do. A raven cawed in the distance. Elwic jerked to hear the familiar and ancient sound. Actar exhaled. Their lives together were coming to an end. The world would change, as it always has and has done for millennia.

The monk watched as the two men stood and embraced. Sullen looks, saturated with love, could not exempt the power of commitment and trust that had been built over time. The separation was a temptation of fate. One would stay where treasures lay, and the other would dig for the future's way.

"What do I say?" Elwic looked at the monk. "How do I address the townspeople who have entrusted me as their guide?"

The monk nodded and pointed to his heart.

The words of Magister rang in his ears: "Seek to be without guile. Know that when you are ready to speak, your words are formed by the spirit of innocence and with the menace of a dragon. Walk in meekness, but carry the sword of truth."

He bowed in reverence. He yielded to the Spirit that spoke to his heart, though he did not understand the shadow coming. The path was hidden until his first step, and then the next. It was as though the journey to the Temple of Wisdom and Truth was never to be won. His journey was to continue no matter the stage he thought he had acquired. He remembered Magister's words, "Wisdom and Truth are the vessels of life. The thirst for these will never be quenched. When you have had your fill, your vessel will fail. Seek to be filled and desire to share the abundance of all you have been gifted to reveal. Empty yourself for the benefit of all, and all will be added unto your own fulfillment."

The task was new. The dawn arrived. The calling was certain. The road ahead was unsure, and yet confidence was the word, faith was the driver, and integrity to what the Spirit was asking would keep Elwic true.

He would face this challenge head-on, armed with the wisdom and the truth he had gained from the Temple. As he prepared for the journey ahead, he felt a renewed sense of purpose. The Tower bell rang three times to bring the people to the circle outside, where for many years lessons, challenges, parables, and stories would teach the virtues handed down from The Temple of Wisdom and Truth.

Elwic announced his time was fulfilled. A voice raised above the crowd, "Will you return?"

Elwic scanned the edge of the gathering and found the monk; the monk's head was bowed in prayer. Though he knew he couldn't rely on the monk for answers, part of him wished he could. Turning back to the sea of expectant faces, he said, "I don't know." He shook his head. "I didn't know if I'd ever return when I first left Havenbrook, yet here I am." A sheepish smile crossed his face.

"Who will teach us until your return?" Another question

from the crowd but this one was filled with a tremble of lips and a haunting gasp of air. Crying could be heard.

Elwic did not want to lie nor give false hope. Actar was standing behind him with a quill and papyrus pad in hand. He was not writing. His tears streamed down both cheeks, soaking the pad with the liquid of his heart, silently etching the burden of his soul for all to see.

Questions poured from the souls of Havenbrook. Murmurs ensued. Elwic raised his hands up and wide from his shoulders. His action hushed the crowd into a respectful silence.

"As the Spirit of Magister has taught me and I have taught you, so your teacher will continue. Though I leave, there are many who are qualified to instruct and guide you. Actar has written my words as I have been directed by Magister. He will remain here as caretaker of the Tower and all the scrolls therein. Today, I bequeath my authority to him and anyone he deems worthy to read and share the words of Magister."

Weeping commenced. Elwic stepped straight away into the center. A narrow path appeared as the folk touched him as he passed through their gauntlet. Actar followed close behind, still holding his writing tools. Elwic broke free from the dusty tunnel of cloth and flesh. His back was broad, and his stare forward was definite. He reached behind his neck with both hands, gathered the hood of woven burlap, and flung it forward. It was a sign he was covering his head and beginning a journey. He did not look back. The monk, now by his side, replicated the action of bringing his hooded apparel in place. Two travelers leaving. A town began grieving. Actar stood motionless at the point of the throng and panted, his heart breaking and his chest heaving.

And so, under the veil of dawn's first light, Elwic took his first steps away from Havenbrook, embarking on a journey that would take him far beyond the familiar, into lands of wonder and peril, where his next destiny awaited. The townspeople watched in reverence, knowing that though he was leaving, the legacy of his deeds would forever be etched in the soul of Havenbrook. Some wept, and some cheered. Actar dropped to his knees and pounded the dirt. He accepted his fate, rather a calling to be true to his master, Elwic the Sage of Havenbrook. He would be faithful and true to the teachings he had penned.

The morning sun illuminated the landscape and the mountains' edge. All eyes stayed fixed on the forms of the two men. Some hoped it was a test; he would turn around, return, and remain inside the boundaries of Havenbrook. Elwic disappeared into the distance, guided by the monk's steady presence and the light of the sun, ready to face whatever the future held.

And so it was that the sage of Havenbrook, the messenger and teacher from the Temple of Wisdom and Truth, embarked on a new journey of faith to seek out and learn from the ONE who called him.

ELWIC AND THE MONK
EPILOGUE

In the quiet hush of Havenbrook's green,
Where past and purpose both had been,
Elwic stood, his journey's end,
A soul once lost, now found again.
The village sighed, with hearts grown dear,
To he who'd lived and conquered fear,
Yet purpose called — a whisper low,
A path unseen, where he must go.
A monk in robes, both young and wise,
Held secrets deep as starry skies.
With eyes that knew of distant lands,
He offered Elwic guiding hands.
"Come forth," he said, "for there lies more
Beyond this quiet, sacred shore.
The world awaits your light to roam,
So leave, and let your soul find home."
Through fields and fog, past brook and glen,
Elwic stepped on, beyond known men.
With Havenbrook held in his heart,
He took his leave — a new world's start.